Once There Was a Story

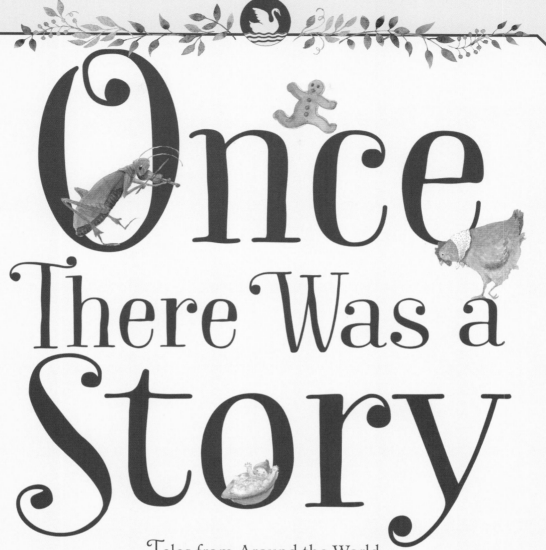

Once There Was a Story

Tales from Around the World, Perfect for Sharing

Jane Yolen

ILLUSTRATED BY

Jane Dyer

A Paula Wiseman Book

SIMON & SCHUSTER BOOKS FOR YOUNG READERS

New York   London   Toronto   Sydney   New Delhi

SIMON & SCHUSTER BOOKS FOR YOUNG READERS
An imprint of Simon & Schuster Children's Publishing Division
1230 Avenue of the Americas, New York, New York 10020
Text copyright © 2017 by Jane Yolen
Illustrations copyright © 2017 by Jane Dyer
All rights reserved, including the right of reproduction in whole or in part in any form.
SIMON & SCHUSTER BOOKS FOR YOUNG READERS is a trademark of Simon & Schuster, Inc.
For information about special discounts for bulk purchases,
please contact Simon & Schuster Special Sales at 1-866-506-1949 or business@simonandschuster.com.
The Simon & Schuster Speakers Bureau can bring authors to your live event.
For more information or to book an event, contact the Simon & Schuster Speakers Bureau
at 1-866-248-3049 or visit our website at www.simonspeakers.com.
Book design by Laurent Linn
The text for this book was set in Minister Std.
The illustrations for this book were rendered in gouache
and colored pencils on Arches 140 pound hot press paper.
Manufactured in China
0917 SCP
2 4 6 8 10 9 7 5 3 1
CIP data for this book is available from the Library of Congress.
ISBN 978-1-4169-7172-6

For Sophia DiTerlizzi, who loves books
—J. Y.

For Rubin Pfeffer and Rick Richter, for believing in this project so many years ago,
Paula Wiseman and Laurent Linn, for the care and creativity they gave this book,
and Jane Yolen, for retelling and writing the stories.
—J. D.

Once
There Was a
Story

CONTENTS

Tales of Magic Makers

How to Love a Story: An Introduction

How to love a story? Read it aloud. Let it melt in the mouth. There is magic between the mouth and ear when a story is involved. Especially if it is your mouth and a child's ear. I know this magic well.

I have loved fairy tales and folktales all my life, and have always read them aloud. They are like little presents that caress the ear, playing on the tympanum, beating the eardrum with their magic messages.

Which tales? When I was a child, I never cared where they came from, only that they found me. What if they were from Europe or the British Isles or the Middle East or the Russias or Asia or Africa or the Americas? What did it matter if they grew up in the hot lands or the cold, the old worlds or the new? What interested me were the stories, all speaking to me of lives lived and life ahead.

When my own children were young, folktales and fairy tales were staples in our house. So when I was discussing this book with my editor, I wanted to be sure some of our old favorites were retold here. That's why you have retellings of many familiar folktales.

But from the time I was young, already immersed in all the colored Fairy Books of Andrew Lang, I acquired an extensive knowledge and love of more than the ordinary and familiar stories, so there are some of those here as well. And two of my own stories to round out the rest. Thirty tales in all.

These are stories that are short, full of remarkable characters, infinitely retellable, and fit for children between three and five years of age. I hope—as you read them with a child on your lap, or snuggling next to you in bed, or sitting with young friends at your feet, their eager faces falling under the story's spell—I hope that you love the stories as well as they do.

—*Jane Yolen*

Homey Tales

THE GINGERBREAD MAN
(America)

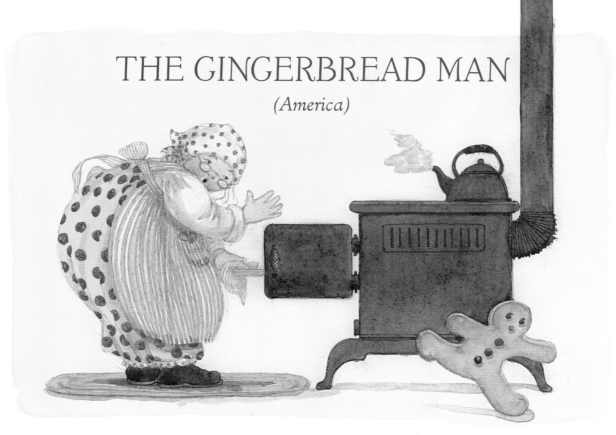

nce upon a time, an old farmer and his wife lived in a little house on the edge of a woods.

That morning as a special treat the wife made a gingerbread man. She mixed the batter, rolled out the dough, and carefully cut out the figure. Then, *pip-pip-pop*, she gave him raisin eyes, a cinnamon-drop mouth, and buttons made of chocolate mints.

My, didn't he look fine!

She set him in the oven to bake.

Soon the kitchen filled with the smell of fresh-baked gingerbread, and the farmer's wife opened the oven door.

Out jumped the gingerbread man!

Away he went, through the front door and across the yard. Behind him came the farmer's wife waving her wooden spoon and the farmer waving his pitchfork.

"Stop, stop," they cried. "We want to eat you."

The gingerbread man looked over his shoulder and called out,

"Run, run, as fast as you can,
You can't catch me, I'm the gingerbread man."

Well, the farmer and his wife tried and tried, but indeed they couldn't catch him.

As the gingerbread man went by the sty, a pig looked up and wrinkled its snout. "Oink," it said. "Slow down. I want to eat you."

The gingerbread man laughed. "I've run away from the farmer and the farmer's wife, and I shall run away from you, too."

"But I'm hungry," said the pig.

The gingerbread man shook his head.

"Run, run, as fast as you can,
You can't catch me, I'm the gingerbread man."

And away he ran.

Behind him ran the farmer and the farmer's wife and the pig, but they couldn't catch him.

Soon the gingerbread man passed a horse in the field.

The horse looked up from cropping grass. "Neigh," it said. "Slow down. I want to eat you."

The gingerbread man laughed. "I've run away from the farmer and the farmer's wife, and from the pig. I shall run away from you, too."

"But I'm hungry," said the horse.

The gingerbread man shook his head.

"Run, run, as fast as you can,
You can't catch me, I'm the gingerbread man."

And away he ran. Behind him ran the farmer and the farmer's wife and the pig and the horse, too, but they couldn't catch him.

The gingerbread man ran and ran until he ran all the way through the woods and came to a river. He didn't know how to get across it because he couldn't swim.

Just then along came a sly and hungry fox. "Hmmm," the fox said to itself, "dinner has just walked into my life."

Now the gingerbread man saw the hungry fox and said, "I've run away from the farmer and the farmer's wife, and from the pig, and from the horse, too, and I shall run away from you."

The fox smiled at the gingerbread man but was careful not to show its teeth. "I am sure you're much faster than I am. But I can also see that you do not know how to swim. Jump on my tail, friend, and I will take you across. Once on the other side, you can run away all you like, for I shall not follow."

The gingerbread man saw that the fox's tail was a long way from its mouth, so he jumped on and they started across the river.

Halfway there the fox turned its head just a wee bit and said, "You're much too heavy for my tail, pray jump on my back."

Well, the fox's back was still a long way from its mouth, so the gingerbread man did just that.

But when they were almost to the other side, the fox said, "You're too heavy for my back and in danger of being swamped by the water, so jump onto my nose."

Well, the fox's nose was long and still quite a ways from its mouth, so the gingerbread man did just that.

But as they reached the riverbank, the fox lifted its head, flipped the gingerbread man into the air, opened its mouth—teeth and all—and *snip, snick, snack*, that was the end of the gingerbread man. And the sly fox was no longer hungry.

Running away as fast as you can
May not be the very best lifelong plan.

THE TURNIP
(Russia)

ld Mishka planted a turnip. The turnip grew and grew. It grew so big that it had to be harvested.

So Old Mishka started to pull the turnip out of the ground. He pulled and pulled, but the turnip would not come out.

Old Mishka called over his wife, Old Masha. "Put your arms around me and pull," he said.

Old Masha took hold of Old Mishka. Old Mishka took hold of the turnip. Then they pulled and pulled, but couldn't pull the turnip out.

Old Masha called over her granddaughter, Tasha. "Put your arms around me and pull," she said.

So Tasha took hold of Old Masha. Old Masha took hold of Old Mishka. Old Mishka took hold of the turnip. Then they pulled and pulled, but couldn't pull the turnip out.

Tasha called over the dog, Sasha. "Put your paws around me and pull," she said.

So Sasha took hold of Tasha. Tasha took hold of Old Masha. Old Masha took hold of Old Mishka. Old Mishka took hold of the turnip. Then they pulled and pulled, but couldn't pull the turnip out.

The dog Sasha called over to the cat, Kasha. "Put your paws around me and pull," he said.

So Kasha took hold of Sasha. Sasha took hold of Tasha. Tasha took hold of Old Masha. Old Masha took hold of Old Mishka. Old Mishka took hold of the turnip. Then they pulled and pulled, but couldn't pull the turnip out.

The cat Kasha called over to the mouse, Pishka. "Put your paws around me and pull," she said.

So Pishka took hold of Kasha. Kasha took hold of Sasha. Sasha took hold of Tasha. Tasha took hold of Old Masha. Old Masha took hold of Old Mishka. Old Mishka took hold of the turnip. Then they pulled and pulled, but couldn't pull the turnip out.

The mouse Pishka called over to the flea, Zatka. "Put your legs around me and pull," he said.

So Zatka took hold of Pishka. Pishka took hold of Kasha. Kasha took hold of Sasha. Sasha took hold of Tasha. Tasha took hold of Old Masha. Old Masha took hold of Old Mishka. Old Mishka took hold of the turnip.

Then Zatka, Pishka, Kasha, Sasha, Tasha, Masha, and Mishka pulled and pulled and pulled some more, and . . .

Whoooooooop! The turnip came right out!

Sometimes it takes just one flea more,
Then everyone is on the floor!

LAZY JACK

(England)

Once upon a time, a boy named Jack lived with his mother in a small house. They were poor as poor could be, and his mother made barely enough for the two of them by spinning. But all Jack did was sit outside with the sun on his face in the summer, and sit close to the hearth fire in the winter.

So he was called Lazy Jack by all who knew him.

Now, Monday morning, tired from doing all the work while Jack lazed around, his mother said, "If you do not begin to work for your porridge, my boy, you will have to leave this house for good." And she meant it.

So Jack went out and told a neighboring farmer that he'd work all day for just a penny. In those days a penny was a good wage.

But as Jack had never been given a penny before, he lost it in a brook while going home for supper. Poor Jack.

"You lazy boy!" cried his mother. "You should have put the penny in your pocket."

"I'll do it the next time," said Jack.

The next day, out he went again and hired out to a cowherd, who gave him a jar of milk for his day's work. Remembering what his mother had told him, Jack put the jar in the pocket of his jacket, but of course it was spilled before he got home. Poor Jack.

"You silly boy," said his mother, "you should have carried it balanced on your head."

"I'll do it the next time," said Jack.

Well, the next day he hired out to another farmer. And this one gave him a packet of cream cheese to pay for his work. Remembering what his mother had said, he balanced it on his head. By the time he got home, half the cheese had fallen off and the rest had melted into his hair. Poor Jack.

"You foolish boy," said his mother, "you should have carried it carefully in your hands."

"I'll do it the next time," said Jack.

The very next day Jack hired out to a baker, who gave him a large tomcat for his day's work. Remembering what his mother had told him, he began to carry it home carefully in his hands. But the cat was not happy in his hands, and it scratched Jack so badly, he dropped it by the wayside and the cat ran away. Poor Jack.

"You dippy boy," said his mother, "you should have tied it with a string and dragged it behind you."

"I'll do it the next time," said Jack.

Friday, Jack went to work for a butcher, who paid him well with a handsome steak. Remembering what his mother had told him, Jack tied a string around the meat and dragged it along behind. He pulled it through the dirt, through the mud, and over a briar hedge. By the time he reached his home, the meat was thoroughly spoiled. Poor Jack.

"You ninnyhammer," said his mother, for by now she was quite out of patience, "you should have carried it on your shoulder."

"I'll do it the next time," said Jack.

Well, wouldn't you know it, the next day Jack went to work for a cattle farmer, who gave him a donkey for all his hard work. Remembering what his mother had told him, Jack hoisted the donkey on top of his shoulder, which was very hard to do. And slowly—oh so slowly—he walked back home with his reward.

Now, along the road lived a very rich man who had a beautiful daughter named Jean who'd never laughed and had long since lost her power to speak. Fearing for her life, seven doctors and six nurses all said that if she could but laugh, she would be well again.

At that very moment Jean was gazing out of her window, a sad look on her face, and what did she see but Jack walking by, ever so slowly, with the donkey carried on his shoulder, its legs sticking right up in the air.

It was so funny, she began to laugh . . . and laugh . . . and laugh, so loudly that her father and mother, the seven doctors and six nurses, all came running to see about that strange noise.

"Father, Mother," said Jean, suddenly able to speak again, "look out the window. Have you ever seen anything so funny?"

They all looked, and then they all laughed with Jean. The rich man ran outside at once and brought back Jack, though they left the donkey at the door.

"I will give you anything you wish, for you have saved my daughter's life."

Well, Jack took one look at the rich man's daughter, and he knew what that wish was. Though he wasn't sure if he was to carry her in his pocket, balance her on his head, take her in his hands, tie a string around her, or put her on his shoulder. And when he asked, everyone laughed even more.

"You won't have to take her anywhere," said the rich man. "You can live right here."

So Jack and Jean were married, and he and his mother moved into the big house.

The house rang with laughter from that day till this, and every one of them lived a long and happy life.

To have a happy ever after,
Make sure your house is filled with laughter.

THE LITTLE RED HEN
(England)

Once long ago there was a little red hen who worked all day long in the yard. *Scritch-scratch.*

One day she found a grain of wheat.

If I plant it, it will grow, she thought. Then she turned to her friends. "Who will help me plant the wheat?"

"Not I," said Duck.

"Not I," said Pig.

"Not I," said Dog.

They all preferred playing to work.

"Never mind," said the little red hen, "I shall plant it myself." And she did.

All that summer the wheat grew. First it was a little green shoot, and then it was a great big stalk. Under the summer sun it turned golden yellow.

"Now my wheat is ripe," said the little red hen. "Who will help me cut it?"

"Not I," said Duck.

"Not I," said Pig.

"Not I," said Dog.

They all preferred playing to work.

"Never mind," said the little red hen, "I shall cut it myself." And she did.

Now it was time to thresh the wheat. "Who will help me thresh it?" asked the little red hen.

"Not I," said Duck.

"Not I," said Pig.

"Not I," said Dog.

They all preferred playing to work.

"Never mind," said the little red hen, "I shall thresh it myself." And she did.

Now it was time to take the threshed wheat to the mill. "Who will help me carry it to the mill?" asked the little red hen.

"Not I," said Duck.

"Not I," said Pig.

"Not I," said Dog.

They all preferred playing to work.

"Never mind," said the little red hen, "I shall carry it there myself." And she did.

The miller ground the wheat into the finest flour and the little red hen carted it home. "Who will help me make the bread?" she asked.

"Not I," said Duck.

"Not I," said Pig.

"Not I," said Dog.

They all preferred playing to work.

"Never mind," said the little red hen, "I shall make it myself." And she did.

She mixed the flour with salt and water. She kneaded the dough and pounded it. She shaped it into a loaf. Then she put the loaf into the oven. Soon the smell of baking bread filled the barnyard.

"Who will help me eat the bread?" asked the little red hen.

"I will," said Duck.

"I will," said Pig.

"I will," said Dog.

They all preferred eating to work.

The little red hen shook her head. "You didn't help me plant the wheat or cut it or thresh it or carry it to the mill. You did not help me mix it or knead it or pound it or shape it or bake it in the oven."

She took the bread to her table and sat down. She tied a napkin around her neck. "So I shall eat it all by myself."

And she did.

Share the work each time you meet,
And you will share good things to eat.

THE LITTLE OLD LADY WHO LOST HER DUMPLING

(Japan)

L ong ago there lived a funny old woman who loved to laugh. *Tee-hee-hee!* Also, she was a master at making rice flour.

One day while she was preparing dumplings for dinner, one dumpling fell onto the dirt floor. It rolled and rolled right into a hole and—*plip! plop!*—disappeared.

The old woman put her hand down the hole, but all at once the earth gave way and in she fell too.

She tumbled and tumbled a long way, till she landed with a *bang!* Standing, she saw before her an unknown road.

"Where am I?" She could see many rice fields, but no one worked them. "I must have fallen into another country," she decided, and set forth.

Now the road sloped downward, so she knew her dumpling must have rolled farther away. Off she ran, laughing *tee-hee-hee* and calling out:

> "Dumpling, dumpling, dumpling mine,
> The dumpling on which I shall dine.
> Where is that dumpling?"

After a little while she came to a stone jizo, protector of roads. "O Lord Jizo," she asked, "have you seen my dumpling?"

Jizo answered: "Yes, I saw your dumpling tumbling along. But do not go any farther. A wicked oni lives nearby, and he eats people."

The old woman wasn't afraid of the oni. She laughed, *tee-hee-hee,* and ran on.

Soon she came to another stone jizo. "O Lord Jizo, have you seen my dumpling?"

The jizo said: "Yes, I saw your dumpling go tumbling by. But you must not run any farther. There is a wicked oni nearby who eats people."

The old woman still wasn't afraid of the oni. She laughed, *tee-hee-hee,* and called as she ran on:

> "Dumpling, dumpling, dumpling mine,
> The dumpling on which I shall dine.
> Where is that dumpling?"

She came to a third jizo and asked the same question.

This jizo said: "Hush, woman. Here comes the oni now, and he's *very* hungry! Squat behind my sleeve and don't make any noise."

This time she *was* afraid and did as the jizo commanded.

Boom! Boom! The giant oni came stomping by. He was ten feet high and ten feet wide and very ugly. He bowed to the jizo, then sniffed the air.

"Jizo-san, tell me true,
I smell a human close to you."

"Oh!" said the jizo." Perhaps you are mistaken." A jizo can't lie, but it can be careful.

Sniffing again, the oni said, "Yes indeed, I smell a human."

He was so funny, with his great snout in the air, the old woman couldn't help laughing. *Tee-hee-hee!*

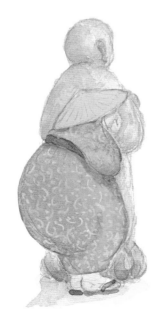

The oni pulled her out from behind the jizo's stone sleeve, and she was still laughing, *tee-hee-hee!*

"That good old woman is under my protection," said the jizo. "You must not hurt her."

"Then I will not *make* her my dinner, but make her *cook* my dinner," said the oni.

So he carried her down the road till they came to a wide river, where there was a boat. There the oni put her into the boat and rowed her across to his house. The house was large, but then, it would be. Onis are very large.

He led the little old woman into the kitchen and told her to cook some dinner, handing her a small wooden rice paddle.

"This is a magic rice paddle. Put only a single grain of rice into a pot of water, and when you stir that single grain with this paddle, it will become many grains, until the pot is full."

Tee-hee-hee! The old woman laughed and did as the oni said. As she stirred the single grain with the paddle, it became two, then four, then eight, then sixteen grains. In less time than it takes to tell, the huge rice pot was full.

After that, the funny old woman cooked food for the oni and his enormous friends every day. Think how big an oni is. Then think of a houseful of onis. That's a *lot* of rice!

Although the oni kept his promise and never ate the little old lady, she was terribly lonely and wanted to be back in her own little house. She even stopped laughing.

So one day when the oni and his friends were all out, she took off her apron and ran away. But first she grabbed the magic paddle and slipped it under her obi sash. Then down to the river she went, where the boat was pulled up on shore.

She pushed the boat into the water, got in, and began to row. Soon she was far from the shore.

But this was a very wide river. The little old lady pulled and pulled on the oars till her back hurt and her hands were raw, and still she wasn't halfway across.

Suddenly the oni and his friends came back to the house, hungry as only onis can be. They discovered that their cook was gone, and with her the magic paddle.

So they ran down to the river at once and saw the old woman rowing away.

Now, onis cannot swim. And the old woman had their only boat.

"I know!" said the oni to his friends. "We can drink up all the water in the river. Then we can just run out and catch her."

It sounded like a good plan. So they knelt down and began to drink as fast as they could, which was very fast indeed.

The water got lower . . .

  And lower . . .

    And lower.

But the old woman kept on rowing until the water became too shallow for the boat, so shallow that the onis stopped drinking. They began to wade across, shaking their fists at her, avoiding the biggest puddles.

The old woman dropped her oars and took the magic paddle from her obi sash. She shook it back at the onis.

They found this so funny, they burst out laughing. *Ho-ho-ho!*

And the very moment they began to laugh, all the water they'd drunk spurted out of their mouths. The river became full again. And remember—onis can't swim.

So the funny old woman got safely over to the other side and—*tee-hee-hee!*—she ran up the road fast and faster until she found herself at home again.

With the magic paddle she made enough rice and rice flour to sell to her neighbors, and in this way became quite a rich old lady. And she lived quite happily—and laughingly—ever after.

Magic paddles making rice
Can make your living awfully nice.

THE BREMEN TOWN MUSICIANS

(Germany/Brothers Grimm)

There was once a donkey who'd carried sacks to and from the mill for years. But now the donkey was too old to work.

"I'm sorry," said the miller, "but you're . . ."

Donkey didn't stay to hear the rest, but ran off as fast as he could. He thought that if he could get to the town of Bremen, he'd become a musician.

A little way along he came upon a hunting dog lying in the road, panting.

"Why are you lying in the road, Grab-Hold?" asked Donkey.

"Because I'm old and can no longer hunt with my master. He was going to kill me, so I ran off. I don't know what I shall do now."

"Well," said Donkey, "I'm going to Bremen to become a musician. Why not come too? I'll play the fiddle, you can beat the drums."

The dog jumped right up, and off they went together.

Soon they came to a cat sitting by the side of the road. Her face looked like three days of bad weather.

"What's bothering you, Mistress Mustache-Licker?" asked the donkey.

"Oh," answered Cat, "I'm getting on in years. I'd rather sit by the fire than chase any mice. So mistress wanted to drown me. But I figured it out before she got her sack, and took off. Now where can I go?"

"Come with us to Bremen," Donkey said. "We're starting a band. After all, you sing in the night."

"What a great idea," purred Cat.

So the three went on along the road till they came to a farmyard. There was a rooster sitting on the gate crying with all his might.

"Wow, that hurts the ears," said Dog.

"Pierces the heart," said Cat.

"What's the matter?" asked Donkey.

"I've served this house for five years calling up the sun, and now they want to serve me—for Sunday dinner!" said Rooster. "All because I've gotten old."

"Hey now, Red-Head," said Donkey, "come away with us to Bremen. We're starting a band. You have a good voice. Well, a loud voice, anyway. I play the fiddle, and Dog the drums. Cat will sing at night. You can sing during the day."

So off they went toward Bremen.

But Bremen was a long way still, and they were just passing through a forest when the sun went down. So they tucked in for the night. Donkey and Dog lay down under a big tree. Cat climbed to the first branch, where she stretched out. And Rooster flew right to the top of the tree, where he would be the first to see the sunrise. He looked around in all four directions and thought he saw a little light in the distance.

"Hey, down below," Rooster called to his new friends. "There's a light ahead. That means a house. It'll be better to sleep in comfort than out in the cold forest."

They all agreed. So off they went till they came to the house.

Donkey looked in the window. He saw a big table set with good things to eat and drink, and several men sitting around it counting out gold and silver goblets, bags of coins, and money boxes that they took out of sacks.

"What do you see, Gray-Horse?" asked Rooster.

"I see a table set with good things to eat and drink, and robbers sitting there enjoying themselves."

"Food!" said Dog.

"Drink!" said Cat.

"Robbers!" said Rooster.

They all came to the window to see for themselves: Dog on Donkey's back, Cat on Dog's back, and Rooster on Cat's head.

"How can we get rid of them?" they whispered to one another.

"With our brave music," Donkey said.

So Donkey brayed, Dog barked, Cat screeched, Rooster crowed. Then they crashed through the window into the room.

The robbers thought the police had come. They jumped up at the terrible music and fled into the woods.

The four hungry musicians seated themselves at the table and ate and ate until there was nothing left.

Then they put out the light and looked for somewhere to sleep. Donkey lay down outside in the hay. Dog settled by the back door. Cat found the hearth with its warm ashes. And Rooster flew up to the roof beam. Tired from their long journey, they were soon asleep.

When midnight came, the robbers saw that the light was no longer burning in the house. Everything seemed quiet.

So the captain said, "Shame on us. We were chased off too easily. Henry, you must go back and see what's going on."

So, off went Henry.

He opened the front door carefully. Everything was quiet. He went to stick a candle into the fire. But instead he mistook the cat's glowing, fiery eye for a live coal (because cats can sleep with one eye open, you know). Cat didn't think this funny at all and jumped into Henry's face, spitting and scratching.

Henry was horribly frightened and ran toward the back door, but Dog jumped up and bit him on the leg.

When Henry tried to escape across the yard past the hay pile, Donkey gave him a nasty kick with his hind foot.

Awakened by the noise, Rooster cried loudly, "Cock-a-doodle-doo!"

Henry ran back to the robbers and said, "Oh, there's an awful witch sitting by the fire who scratched my face with her long fingernails. And a man with a knife standing by the back door who stabbed me in the leg. And a monster lying in the yard who struck me with an iron club. All the while a judge called from on high, 'I want a piece of him too!' I barely got out alive."

Terrified, the robbers ran all the way past Bremen and took the first boat to America.

As for the four musicians, they liked the house so well, they never left it again. For all I know, they're there still.

Music can make robbers cry.
Sing aloud and watch them fly.

TOPS AND BOTTOMS

(Africa/America)

ear and Hare were friends. At least Bear thought so. But Hare knew he was nothing more than Bear's slave.

Every year Bear let Hare use his land to grow enough food for the long, cold winter. They were supposed to share as equals. But every year Bear took almost everything that Hare grew. And Bear was so big, Hare was afraid to complain. The one time he had, Bear had boxed his ears.

"This cannot go on," Hare told his wife. "This year things will have to be different."

"What can you do?" said his wife. "If he takes away the little bit of the crop he lets us have, we'll surely starve."

"I'll think of something," said Hare. So he sat down and thought and thought, and finally went to Bear's house and knocked on the door.

Sleepily, Bear called out, "Come in."

"This year," Hare said, "I'll let you have either the tops or the bottoms of everything I plant, and no complaints."

"No complaints?" asked Bear. "I like the sound of that. But I don't exactly trust you. Who chooses?"

"You do," said Hare.

"Tops!" Bear said, and went back to sleep.

So Hare planted carrots and more carrots, all over Bear's field. The carrots sprouted early, and soon the field was covered with the feathery greens.

Bear strolled by. He saw how tall the green was growing. "I still get all the tops," he said.

"You bet," said Hare, "as long as I get all the bottoms."

"It's a promise," said Bear.

But at harvest time Hare pulled out the carrots that grew under the ground and kept them. He sold half the carrots, and he and his wife had the rest for dinner all winter long. Bear got the feathery tops, and he was not pleased.

"You fooled me," he said, growling. It was a deep growl and very scary. "It won't happen again. Next year I get all the bottoms!"

"Okay," said Hare. "As long as I get all the tops."

"Done," said Bear. They shook paws, and Bear went off to sleep.

But that spring Hare planted snap beans that grew on vines. They grew so quickly and so fast, he had to build a lattice fence for them. The vines twined around the fence, growing toward the light.

When it was time for harvest, Hare gathered all the beans. He sold half the beans, and he and his wife had the rest to eat all winter long. He left the roots for Bear.

Bear was not pleased. "You fooled me again," he said, growling. He had a scary growl. And many sharp teeth. "It won't happen again. Next year I get both tops and bottoms."

"Okay," said Hare, "as long as I get what is in between."

"Done," said Bear. They shook paws, and Bear went off to sleep.

That spring Hare planted field corn. The roots went deep, and the stalks grew high. Bear came by and inspected what grew, both tops and bottoms, and was pleased.

At harvesttime Hare cut down the stalks. He gave Bear the roots. "Bottoms," he said.

He gave Bear the green stalks.

"Tops," he said.

"And I get the in-betweens," he said, which meant he took all of the ears of corn for himself. He sold half the corn, and he and his wife had the rest to eat all winter long.

Bear was not pleased. He growled and showed his teeth, but there was nothing he could do. Hare had done only what he had said he would do, and Bear had agreed to it. Bear went to sleep hungry that winter.

As for Hare, he'd made so much money with his carrots, beans, and corn that he bought his own field the next spring and planted whatever he wanted. And he and his wife lived happily ever after on their crops.

Whether you are a hare or a man,
The word "plant" always begins with a plan.

THE OLD WOMAN AND HER PIG
(England)

Once an old woman was sweeping her house, and she found a little sixpence. "What shall I do with this coin?" she asked herself. And then she knew. "I'll go to market and buy a little pig. I'd like the company."

And she did.

But as she was coming home, she came to a stile. "Up and over, Piggy," she said. But the piggy wouldn't go over the stile.

So the old woman went a little farther and came to a dog. She said to the dog: "Dog, bite Pig. Piggy won't go over the stile, and if he doesn't, I shan't get home for supper."

But the dog wouldn't.

So she went farther still, and she met a stick. She said: "Stick, Stick, beat Dog. Dog won't bite Pig; Piggy won't go over the stile. And if he doesn't, I shan't get home for supper."

But the stick wouldn't.

She went farther still, and she met a fire. So she said: "Fire, Fire, burn Stick. Stick won't beat Dog; Dog won't bite Pig; Piggy won't go over the stile. And if he doesn't, I shan't get home for supper."

But the fire wouldn't.

She went farther still, and she met some water. So she said: "Water, Water, quench Fire. Fire won't burn Stick; Stick won't beat Dog; Dog won't bite Pig; Piggy won't go over the stile. And if he doesn't, I shan't get home for supper."

But the water wouldn't.

She went farther still, and she met an ox. So she said: "Ox, Ox, drink Water. Water won't quench Fire; Fire won't burn Stick; Stick won't beat Dog; Dog won't bite Pig; Piggy won't go over the stile. And if he doesn't, I shan't get home for supper."

But the ox wouldn't.

She went a little farther, and she met a butcher. So she said: "Butcher, Butcher, kill Ox. Ox won't drink Water; Water won't quench Fire; Fire won't burn Stick; Stick won't beat Dog; Dog won't bite Pig; Piggy won't go over the stile. And if he doesn't, I shan't get home for supper."

But the butcher wouldn't.

She went farther still, and she met a rope. So she said: "Rope, Rope, hang Butcher. Butcher won't kill Ox; Ox won't drink Water; Water won't quench Fire; Fire won't burn Stick; Stick won't beat Dog; Dog won't bite Pig; Piggy won't go over the stile. And if he doesn't, I shan't get home for supper."

But the rope wouldn't.

She went farther still, and she met a rat. So she said: "Rat, Rat, gnaw Rope. Rope won't hang Butcher; Butcher won't kill Ox; Ox won't drink Water; Water won't quench Fire; Fire won't burn Stick; Stick won't beat Dog; Dog won't bite Pig; Piggy won't go over the stile. And if he doesn't, I shan't get home for supper."

But the rat wouldn't.

She went farther still, and she met a cat. So she said: "Cat, Cat, kill Rat. Rat won't gnaw Rope; Rope won't hang Butcher; Butcher won't kill Ox; Ox won't drink Water; Water won't quench Fire; Fire won't burn Stick; Stick won't beat Dog; Dog won't bite Pig; Piggy won't go over the stile. And if he doesn't, I shan't get home for supper."

But the cat said to her, "If you go to yonder cow and fetch me a saucer of milk, I will kill the rat." So away went the old woman to the cow.

But the cow said to her: "If you will go to yonder haystack and fetch me a handful of hay, I'll give you the milk."

So away went the old woman to the haystack, and she brought the hay to the cow.

As soon as the cow had eaten up all the hay, she gave the old woman the milk.

Well, away went the old woman with the milk in a saucer to give to the cat.

The cat lapped up the milk, and then . . . the cat began to kill the rat; the rat began to gnaw the rope; the rope began to hang the butcher; the butcher began to kill the ox; the ox began to drink the water; the water began to quench the fire; the fire began to burn the stick; the stick began to beat the dog; the dog began to bite the pig; the pig in a fright jumped over the stile. Everyone stopped what they were doing, so the old woman got home in time for supper.

A bit of a threat is just enough
When things get hard and the hardy get tough.

STONE SOUP
(France/Portugal)

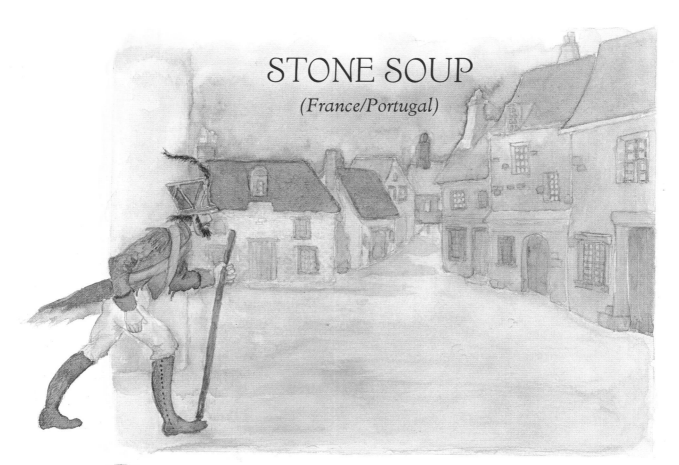

O nce upon a time, a soldier marched wearily home from the war. *Hup . . . and one. Hup . . . and two.*

He had not eaten in days.

Suddenly, up ahead, he saw the lights of a small village and thought, *Surely I can find food and a bed there for the night.*

He began to march with a more hopeful step—*hup, hup, hup*—down the road.

When he got to the village and no one came to greet him, he quickly understood. They were afraid of soldiers and as tired of the war as he. They'd hidden all their food and closed their doors.

The soldier was right. The villagers had sacks of barley stuck in the haylofts. Buckets of milk had been lowered into the well. All their potatoes and carrots and cabbages and beans were in the cellars, hidden behind barrows. Any meat had been hidden in closets under their clothes.

But the soldier was too hungry to go on. So when he finally saw an old woman peering out her window, he said, "Please, madam, can you spare a bit to eat for a starving man?"

"No food here!" the woman cried, and shut her window with a crash.

The soldier went to the next house. "Can you feed a hungry man?" he asked.

The farmer and his wife turned their backs. "Bad harvest," they said.

He went from house to house, but it was the same—the butcher, the baker, the cooper, the dairyman, the priest—no one had food to share.

So the soldier went to the town square and called out in the loud voice he used on the battlefield:

"I KNOW YOU HAVE NO FOOD, SO LET ME COOK YOU MY SPECIAL STONE SOUP."

"Stone soup?"

"Stone soup!"

The villagers were astounded. How on earth could anyone cook soup using a stone? Slowly, by ones and twos and threes, they came out of their houses, until every one of them was standing in a circle in the town square.

Madame Sisle, the best cook in the village, stood with her hands on her hips. "This," she said, "I should like to see."

"And that you will, madam," said the soldier, "if you will but lend me a large kettle for the cooking."

So Madame Sisle sent her son Marcel off to get the pot.

When he came back carrying it over one broad shoulder, the soldier said, "Now we shall need some water, but as that is free, it should not tax your village a bit."

"I will fetch it," said a farmer.

"And I," said another.

They returned quickly with enough water to fill the kettle to the brim.

The soldier sent all the boys off to bring in wood from the forest, and when they came back with armloads, he took out his tinderbox and started the fire. Soon the water in the kettle was bubbling away.

"And now for a proper stone."

The little girls scrabbled around and found any number of stones. The soldier chose three, polished each one on his sleeve, then dropped them—*plip, plup, plop*—into the boiling water.

He sniffed and rubbed his belly. "Ah . . . ," he said, "soon we will have stone soup." Then he thought a minute. "Though it would be greatly improved by some salt and some pepper. And maybe a few herbs."

"I have those," said Madame Sisle, and she sent Marcel back into her kitchen.

"And if you like," the soldier said, "stone soup can be improved even further by a few carrots."

The cooper said, "I have a few." He ran off to fetch them.

When herbs and salt, when pepper and carrots had all been added, the soldier took another taste.

"Getting there," he said. "But . . ." His head cocked to one side, he said thoughtfully, "A cabbage and some potatoes would have made it even better. But as there are none . . ."

"I have a cabbage," said the cooper's wife.

"And I, potatoes," said the baker's wife.

"And I," said the priest, "have some onions, though you haven't mentioned them."

And off they went to bring back their bounty.

Soon the soup smelled so good that everyone crowded in close.

But the butcher's wife took a spoon and tasted the soup. "It is still missing something," she said. "I will find you a large soup bone. Maybe two, since that is such a large kettle."

"Just the thing," said the soldier. "I hardly dared to ask."

And in went not one and not two, but three soup bones, and soon the stone soup was pronounced done.

A table was brought out to the square, and a tablecloth. Soup bowls were set around. The dairyman brought milk in pitchers, and cups. Then they all sat down for a beautiful feast.

"Isn't it amazing," said the priest by way of a blessing, "that all this started with just a few stones."

The soldier smiled. "It's all in knowing how to make it," he said. "And having good friends to help."

A stone in the pot, a helpful hand,
And everything will go as planned.

ROSECHILD
(Jane Yolen)

There lived an old woman who longed for a child, though she was neither widow nor wed.

One day, out in the woods gathering herbs, she heard a cry. There was nothing nearby but a flowering bush, so she went over to that. There, nestled in the petals of a wild rose, was a tiny babe.

Quickly the old woman picked up the child between her forefinger and thumb, and wrapping it in her linen handkerchief, she brought it home. There she made it a cradle from a walnut and lined the shell with soft wool. Then she sat back and wondered how to make such a child grow.

If it were a real child, she thought, *I would feed it pieces of bread sopped in honey and milk till it was quite grown. But as it is a Rosechild, goodness alone knows what I must do, for I do not.*

At last she got up and went to her neighbor Farmer Brow. For surely if anyone would know about raising a child born in a flower, a farmer would. So she knocked on his door, and when Brow opened it, she said,

> "Farmer Brow, tell me now,
> How shall my Rosechild grow?"

Farmer Brow scratched up under his hat and said, "Turn its soil and water it well," for he thought she meant a flowering bush.

So the old woman went home and turned the child in its cradle and sprinkled water upon it from the well. Then she sat down to watch the child for a day, but the Rosechild did not grow.

The next day the old woman got up and went to her other neighbor, Squire Bray. For surely if anyone would know how to raise a child born in a flower, a squire would, for squires know everything. So she knocked on his door, and when he answered it, she said,

> "Squire Bray, tell me the way
> To make my Rosechild grow."

Squire Bray struck his riding crop against his boot and said, "Feed it mash and turn it out to pasture," for he thought she was talking about a horse.

So the old woman went home and fed the Rosechild a meal of mash and put it into the pasture. Then she settled down on the grass beside it and watched for a day, but the Rosechild did not grow.

At last she brought it home again, and when it was asleep in its walnut cradle, she went across the road to the church to see the village priest, Father Bree. For surely if anyone would know how to raise a child born in a flower, a priest would, for he knew about all sorts of strange things in and out of the world. So she knocked on his door, and when he opened it, she said,

> "Father Bree, tell to me,
> How shall my Rosechild grow?"

Father Bree fingered his beads and said, "Place it on the Good Book and make a cross on its forehead," for he feared the old woman was beset by a devil.

So the old woman went home and placed the child on the Good Book and made a cross on its forehead. Then she settled down to watch it for the rest of the day. But still the Rosechild did not grow.

However, there was no one left to ask, so the old woman threw her apron up over her head and cried,

"Oh me, oh my,
My Rosechild shall die."

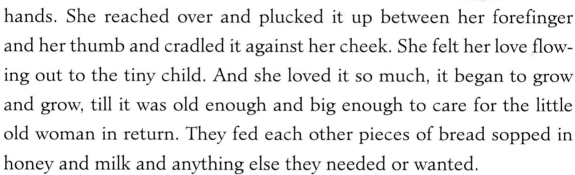

Just then a small, wee voice called out from the walnut shell, "Mama!"

The old woman took her apron off her head and saw the Rosechild holding up its tiny hands. She reached over and plucked it up between her forefinger and her thumb and cradled it against her cheek. She felt her love flowing out to the tiny child. And she loved it so much, it began to grow and grow, till it was old enough and big enough to care for the little old woman in return. They fed each other pieces of bread sopped in honey and milk and anything else they needed or wanted.

And from that day till this, the old woman's house was filled with the lovely scent of roses.

Love is what a growing child needs,
Even one that's grown from seeds.

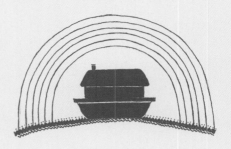

The Very Best Beastly Tales

THE LION AND THE MOUSE

(Greece/Aesop)

ong, long ago, in far-off Africa, a great lion dozed in the sun. Yes, he was proud, but all lions are proud. He was handsome, but all lions are handsome. He was strong, but all lions are strong. And he snored.

Suddenly, by accident, a frightened a little mouse bumped into his nose and woke the proud, strong, handsome lion. Without thinking, the lion imprisoned the mouse in his paw.

"Squeak!" said the mouse, more frightened than before. "Please forgive me, oh Glorious Majesty." For the lion, you know, is considered the king of the jungle. "I know you could squish me and squash me with one move of your paw." And it was true. They both knew it.

But the mouse had something the lion did not: sharp brains. Mice need them, and lions, for the most part, do not.

"How noble indeed you would be, Majesty," said the mouse, "if you acted with mercy and let me go. Then one day I could do you a good deed in turn."

The lion laughed at this and showed many sharp teeth. "Well, I hardly think a mouse can help a lion," he said, "but as I am feeling noble today, I *will* let you go." He opened his big paw and then fell right back to sleep.

"Oh, thank you, Majesty, and I will return the favor if I can," said the little mouse.

But the lion did not hear her above his own snores.

Not too long after that, the lion was roaming the forest, not really watching where he was going, lions rarely do, and he walked right into a net that had been set out by hunters who wanted to sell a lion to a big zoo in a faraway city.

The lion roared and roared, but that did him no good. Nets have no ears, and lion hunters have no pity.

Many of the animals in the jungle heard him roar, but the only one who came to see what it was about was the little mouse.

Ah, she thought, *a promise made must be honored.*

"Your Majesty," she squeaked, though he could not hear her over his own roars.

But when he finally stopped to take a deep breath, she said it again. "Your Majesty . . ."

He peered through the ropes that held him and saw the little mouse.

"As you took pity on me, I will take pity on you. One noble act for another." And the mouse began to gnaw on the netting, until she'd made a hole large enough for the lion to escape.

From that day to this, the lion has been good to small creatures. Who knows when he might need someone's help again? As for the little mouse—she's careful where she runs. Not all big, toothy animals are noble, after all.

A lion, a mouse, a resolution,
A promise kept, a net solution.

THE MEAN TIGER AND THE HARE
(Korea)

When tigers still lived in the Korean hills, there was an especially mean tiger. The older he got, the meaner he got, especially when he was hungry.

And he was *always* hungry.

One day Mean Tiger came across a little hare gathering fresh grass for dinner.

Mean Tiger growled, "I'm hungry and I'm going to eat you!"

Now, Little Hare knew that running away would do him no good. Mean Tiger was bigger, stronger, and faster than he was. Little Hare would have to outthink him.

So he said, "Dear Uncle Tiger, I've been waiting for you. I've some delicious food down in the valley. Just follow me."

Mean Tiger thought, *I'll eat his delicious food and then eat him after.*

As they walked along, Little Hare picked up small, round stones and put them in his sack.

"Why are you putting stones in your sack?" asked Mean Tiger.

"They're delicious baked, I call them hard cakes," said Little Hare. "I have ten for our dinner—five for you, five for me."

Mean Tiger wanted all ten for himself.

Once in the valley, Little Hare started a fire. When it was aroar, he put the stones in.

Mean Tiger watched hungrily.

Little Hare said, "I'll get some fine bean sauce of Mother's. It will make the cakes taste even better. Don't eat any till I return."

Mean Tiger counted the stone cakes in the fire and saw there were eleven and not ten. He thought: *Little Hare won't notice if I eat just that one.* He reached in, brought out the hot stone, and swallowed it greedily. It burned his mouth and tongue, and he leaped up and ran around crying out loud. It took him a month before he could eat anything again.

Once he was mended, Mean Tiger was meaner than before. And hungrier than before. He growled and howled around the hills. Eventually he found Little Hare again, standing near a bush in the middle of a field where there were hundreds of sparrows flying about.

"You tricked me," he roared. "I haven't been able to eat for a month. So now I'm going to eat *you*."

Little Hare knew he'd fooled Mean Tiger once. But could he do it

twice? He thought and thought. Then he said, "If you'd waited for the bean sauce, you wouldn't have burned your mouth, Uncle Tiger. But I forgive you. See all these sparrows? I'm catching them for you."

Deep in his heart Mean Tiger knew Little Hare was right. He hadn't waited for the bean sauce. And there *were* hundreds of sparrows. What a grand meal that would be. Afterward he would eat Little Hare, too.

"Look up at the sky, Uncle Tiger," said Little Hare. "Open your mouth. I'll drive the sparrows right in, and you won't even have to chew."

Well, Mean Tiger's teeth had gotten very loose after a month of not eating, so he sat right down next to the bush, opened his mouth, and waited.

Then Little Hare called out, "Here they come, Uncle Tiger. Better close your eyes so they don't hurt you." But all the while he was setting the bush on fire.

To Mean Tiger, the *crack-crack-crackle* of the flames sounded like hundreds of birds twittering. By the time he finally opened his eyes, his fur was aflame.

He leaped up, his beautiful fur coat burning down to his skin. He had to stay in his cave for a month till it grew back, because otherwise the other animals would laugh at him.

A month later it was winter. Mean Tiger's fur had finally grown back. He went into the valley, stalking about the farms, looking for cattle to eat, but they'd all been locked in barns.

So he went down to the river, thinking about fish but not knowing how to catch any.

There by the riverbank was Little Hare.

"You rascal!" shouted Mean Tiger. "This time I'm eating you for sure."

Little Hare thought even more quickly than before. "I'm glad you found me, Uncle Tiger, because if you're truly hungry, the river is full of fish this time of year."

Mean Tiger roared. "I don't know how to catch fish, but I do know how to catch little hares."

Little Hare answered, "I'd be honored to teach you, Uncle."

"Are you trying to fool me again?"

"I didn't fool you before. It was your own greed that did you in."

Well, Mean Tiger had to agree there was some truth in that, so he nodded. "All right."

Little Hare said, "Do you see my scruffy tail? I dip it into the water and catch one fish at a time. But with your beautiful long tail, you'll be able to catch many fish more."

"With my *tail*?"

"If a little hare can do such a thing, a magnificent tiger can do even better."

So Mean Tiger dipped his tail into the cold water, thinking: *There will be many fish today. And hare after.* So he waited, tail in the water, while Little Hare waded downriver to scare the fish toward him.

Little Hare called out, "I know it's cold, but think of all the fish I'm sending upstream. So many will grab your tail, it will begin to feel very heavy."

Sure enough his tail began to feel very, *very* heavy. But what he didn't know was that as the sun went down, the river water had frozen all around his tail.

"Lift your tail, Uncle," cried Little Hare. "You must have many fish now."

But of course it was not the fish who were caught. It was Mean Tiger.

Early next morning the villagers found Mean Tiger. They put a rope around his neck, put him in a cage, and took him to a zoo. And he never troubled Little Hare again.

Meanness finds its own reward
When your tail's stiff as a board.

THE GRASSHOPPER
AND THE ANT
(Greece/Aesop)

In a green field one summer's day Grasshopper was hopping about, chirping and singing to his heart's content. He fiddled and danced and enjoyed the sun.

Ant passed by carrying a huge golden kernel of corn. He was taking it to the nest.

"Why not come and chat with me?" sang out Grasshopper. "It's a beautiful day. Don't waste it with carrying and worrying."

Ant didn't stop, but said as he passed, "I'm helping to lay up food for the winter." He looked over his shoulder. "And I suggest you do the same."

Grasshopper played another little tune. "Fiddle-i-fee," he sang. "Why bother about winter? It's a long way off. Look at the sun. Feel the soft breeze. Let me sing you a song."

But Ant was already far away.

Grasshopper called after him, "I've got plenty of food. Just look around."

Ant was out of sight.

As for Grasshopper, out of sight meant out of mind, and he immediately forgot all about carrying and worrying, and played yet another tune.

However, summer turned to fall, and fall—as it always happens—became winter.

In winter Grasshopper had no food.

He tried to play a tune or to dance or fiddle, but all he could think of was how his belly ached and how the cold made him shiver. Who was worrying now?

One winter's day Grasshopper saw Ant giving out corn and grain to all the other ants. He went over to them, hopping and hoping. "May I have a bit to eat?"

The ants all looked at him and laughed. "Why not fiddle for your food?" they told him. "Sing for it!"

"Why not *work* for it?" said Ant.

And so, with a much humbled heart, Grasshopper did.

Sing and dance your days away,
But someday soon you'll have to pay.

THE UGLY DUCKLING
(Denmark/Hans Christian Andersen)

Once upon a time in old Denmark, Mother Duck had been sitting on a clutch of new eggs.

She had been at it for some time. And then, one morning, the eggs began to hatch. *Scritch, scratch, snap,* and out popped six lively, pretty yellow ducklings.

But one egg was bigger than all the rest, and that egg didn't hatch.

Mother Duck couldn't remember laying that seventh egg.

"Did I miscount?" she wondered, and turned to take care of her six ducklings who were already running about and making all kinds of demands.

But all of a sudden, with a loud *scritch, scratch, snap,* the last egg finally hatched. And out of it stepped a very strange-looking duckling with gray feathers and an odd-colored beak.

Mother Duck shook her head. "What an ugly duckling! How can it possibly be one of mine!"

It was true. The gray duckling wasn't pretty, and he certainly ate far more than his brothers. Besides, he was very, very clumsy. No one wanted to play with him or eat near him, or even talk to him. In fact, all the farmyard folk simply laughed at him. He felt sad and lonely and more and more unhappy.

Mother Duck did her best to cheer him up, but it was a poor best at that. "Sorry little ugly duckling!" she said. "Why are you so different from the others?"

Of course, that made the ugly duckling feel even worse.

So the very next day, at sunrise, the ugly duckling ran away.

He waddled and waddled until he came to a pond. He asked all the pond birds, "Do you know of any ducklings with gray feathers like mine?"

"We don't know anyone as ugly as you," they said, which made him feel so bad, he walked on to another pond, where a pair of geese gave him the same answer to his question.

And so he went, from pond to forest to farm and back again, but no one had an encouraging word.

Then one day, at dawn, he found himself in a thick bed of reeds. He thought it a good place to hide. There was plenty of food, and the duckling began to feel a little happier, though he was still, of course, very lonely.

Overhead he saw a flight of beautiful birds who were a brilliant white, with long, slender necks, yellow beaks, and large wings. They were migrating south.

If only I could look like them, just for a day! thought the duckling admiringly. But wishes hardly ever change a thing.

Winter came and the water in the reedbed froze. The poor duckling had to leave that place to search for food. He waddled and waddled until he dropped, exhausted, to the ground. He thought: *This is it. This is the end of me.*

But luckily, a farmer found him and put him in his jacket pocket. "I'll take him home to my children to look after."

At the farmer's home, for the first time, the ugly duckling was showered with kindness and able to survive the bitterly cold winter.

By springtime, though, the ugly duckling was so big, the farmer set him free by the pond.

The ugly duckling felt a great urge to float in the water. When he got in, he looked down. The pond was so clear, he could see himself reflected as if in a glass.

"Goodness!" he said aloud. "How I've changed! I hardly recognize myself! Who knew a year would make such a difference?"

A flight of swans winging north glided onto the pond. They swam over to the ugly duckling.

"You're a swan just like us!" they said warmly. "Where have you been hiding?"

A swan? he thought. And then he understood. He'd never been ugly at all. Just . . . just different. "It's a long story," he replied, his elegant, long neck curving. He swam majestically out to the other swans.

And so it was that the very next day he heard children on the riverbank exclaim: "Look at that young swan! He's the handsomest of them all!"

And he almost burst with happiness.

Once the ugly duckling's gone,
You might turn out to be a swan!

THE TORTOISE AND THE HARE

(Greece/Aesop)

Once upon a time, there lived a hare who was extremely proud of his speed. He boasted about it whenever he could. "Watch me go!" he'd say. "No one can beat me!"

Soon no one wanted to be Hare's friend.

Tortoise was slow, maybe the slowest animal there was. But he was the only one to speak up. "Prove . . . it," he said in his slow way. "Let's . . . race. . . ."

Hare smiled. Hare giggled. Hare laughed in a huge and nasty way. "Race you? Why, you're the forest slowpoke, Mr. Get-There-Tomorrow."

"Fast talk is not fast walk," said Tortoise.

So with the help of the other forest folk, they fixed a time and place for the race.

When the day came, it was sunny. Everyone was there to watch.

Hare and Tortoise got to the starting gate at more or less the same time, Hare a bit early, Tortoise a bit late.

The starter's gun went off, and so did Hare. Tortoise did some deep knee bends to warm up, and in that minute Hare had raced out of sight.

Looking back over his shoulder, Hare realized that Tortoise was not following him, so he decided to take a nap. *Even with a nap, I'll still be a lap ahead,* he thought before he fell asleep in the sun.

Tortoise was slow, but he was steady. Putting one foot in front of the other foot in front of the other and the other, he made his careful way around the track. When he came to the first bend, there was Hare fast asleep.

Tortoise tiptoed around him. One foot in front of another in front of another and another till he was out of sight.

Later that afternoon Hare woke from his nap and looked back down the road toward the starting gate. Tortoise was still nowhere to be seen.

"Ha, ha, ha!" said Hare. "No Tortoise anywhere, what a plodder." He got up, stretched, and began to run. He ran fast, he raced the wind, his ears nearly pinned back against his neck by his speed.

But when he went around the final bend in the track, what should he see but Tortoise about to cross the finish line.

Hare stepped up the pace. He was a *whoooooosh* and a *ruuuuuuuush,* but he couldn't get there in time.

That is how Tortoise won the race, and Hare could never again boast about his speed.

Slow and steady sets the pace;
Slowpokes all can win the race.

THE CITY MOUSE AND THE COUNTRY MOUSE

(Greece/Aesop)

Once a city mouse went to visit his cousin in the country carrying his elegant suitcase packed with his silk shirts and high button shoes.

The country mouse was a rough sort. His coat was a shaggy tweed, and his tail was poorly kept. He lived in a hole in the floorboard of an old house and ate only beans and bacon, bread and good yellow cheese. It was poor food, but he was happy.

Still, the city mouse loved his cousin, and the country mouse did everything to make his city cousin welcome. He showed his cousin all the country pleasures. They had long walks down country lanes, paddled about in a small boat on a river, and fished with a pin made into a hook from the side of a stream.

But after a week of this the city mouse had had enough. He twisted his sleek tail through his paws and said, "I cannot understand, Cousin, how you can put up with such poor food. And walking down lanes and paddling about in boats and fishing are so boring. Come visit me instead and I will show you how to live. We have feasts and fetes, bright lights and sparkling cider. When you have been in the city with me for a week, you will wonder how you ever stood the country life."

So the country mouse brushed his teeth and packed his little tote sack, and off they went to the city mouse's house late that night. The house was all lit up, and everything was shiny and new there.

"You will want something to eat after our long journey," the city mouse said, and took his cousin into the grand dining room. A huge chandelier full of twinkly glass hung high above them.

On the great dining-room table they found the remains of a fine feast—cakes and biscuits, chicken and roasts, three kinds of bread and seven kinds of cheeses, some yellow, some white, and some with interesting bits.

They'd just begun to sample the food when they heard a barking and mewing, loud and close.

"What is that?" asked the country mouse.

"Only the dogs of the house," answered the city mouse. "And the cat."

"Only!" cried the country mouse. "I don't like that kind of music played at my dinner."

At that very moment the door flew open. In came two huge bulldogs and a large golden cat.

"Run!" cried the city mouse.

"I'm running!" cried his cousin, grabbing up his tote sack.

They scampered down the tablecloth and into a nearby mousehole, where they trembled and shook after their near escape.

At last the country mouse calmed himself. "Good-bye, Cousin," he said, heading out the back door.

"What—going so soon?"

"Yes," the country mouse replied. "Better beans and bacon and one kind of bread and cheese in peace, than cakes and roasts in fear."

Eating a lot fulfills some dreams;
Eating in peace, some others, it seems.

PLIP, PLOP
(Tibet)

In ancient Tibet three rabbits lived by a lake, and one day the biggest, largest, ripest fruit on a nearby tree fell into the water and made a huge noise.

PLIP, PLOP!

Well, the rabbits didn't know who had made that noise, and thinking it was the sound of a scary beast, they ran off as fast as they could. *Lippity-loppity.*

Who should see them running but a fox, and he called out, "Ho, little brothers, what's wrong?"

They called back over their shoulders, "Plip-Plop is coming, and he will eat us all."

The fox might have been sly, but he was not necessarily smart, and so he, too, began to run frantically, his long red tail straight out behind him. *Slippity-slappety.*

A monkey saw him running. "What is wrong?" called the monkey.

"Plip-Plop is coming, and he will eat us all," the fox cried, never slowing down.

Well, the monkey might have been handy, but she wasn't too smart either. She began to run too. *Handily-pandily.*

And then didn't the other animals fall in line after them: the black bear and brown bear, the leopard, the elephant, the tiger, and even the water buffalo, who was not usually afraid of anything. They ran and they ran, and the more they ran, the scareder they got, till they were outrunning their own shadows and night was coming on.

At last they came to the end of the path, and there stood a lion, his long mane blowing in the wind. He roared at the galloping animals, which stopped them all in their tracks, even the water buffalo.

"Why," asked the lion, "are you all running *helter-skelter* and *handily-pandily* and *slippity-slappity* and *lippity-loppity,* so fast you are outrunning your own shadows?"

The water buffalo said in his slow voice, "Plip-Plop is coming."

And the tiger said, "He will eat us all."

"What, *all* of you?" asked the lion. "I think he would get himself a tummy ache if he ate *all* of you! And who is this Plip-Plop, anyway, and what does he look like?"

Well, those were questions none of them could answer.

"We didn't actually see him, but we heard him," said the rabbits, and everyone knows that rabbits have very good ears.

"Show me this Plip-Plop," said the lion, "and I will eat *him* first!"

So, timidly, the rabbits took the lion back along the path with all of the other animals walking quietly behind, even the water buffalo, who found it very hard to be quiet.

And soon they came to the lake, and the rabbits pointed. "There!" they said.

And just as they pointed, another very ripe fruit, even bigger than the first, fell into the lake.

PLIP, PLOP!

"There!" cried the rabbits. "Did you hear?"

The lion laughed and laughed, which sounded very like his roar. "Silly rabbits, to be frightened by a piece of ripe fruit. But the rest of you are sillier still, to be frightened by a story. I will take this fruit home and eat it myself, the terrible Plip-Plop."

And he did.

Sometimes something that we hear
Brings out the worst thing that we fear.

THE HEN AND
THE BIG, BAD FOX
(Ireland)

Once a plump little hen lived in a house all by herself and she was quite content.

Now, over the hill in a dark, dank den lived a fox, and with him his old snarly, gnarly mother. And they were never content at all. They were hungry and cold and wet, and they complained to each other day and night.

One day the fox heard about the plump little hen, and he said to his mother, "Oh mother of mine, there's a plump little hen lives over the hill. Why don't I go down there and fetch her for our supper?"

"Mind that you do, oh son of mine, and don't go gnawing on her bones before you bring her back." For she didn't trust her son, no she didn't. And he didn't trust her, either.

But though the fox thought and thought about the hen and tried to catch her one, two, and three times, she was much too clever for him. Whenever she went out of her house, she locked the door behind her, *snick-snack*. And every time she went into her house, she locked the door behind her, *snick-snack*. She always kept her key in her pocket, along with her scissors and a piece of sugar candy. What a clever little hen.

So each time the fox had to slink back to his den, where his mother called him names, and they both had to go to bed hungry, which didn't make them happy.

Finally the fox thought up a really rascally plan, and early the next morning he said to his mother, "Oh mother of mine, have the pot boiling, for when I come home, I shall have a plump little hen to put in it."

And though his mother didn't believe him entirely, she put the pot on to boil.

Then out went the fox, his tote bag slung over his shoulder, and he slunk along till he got to the little hen's house. There he hid behind the woodpile to wait.

Just then the little hen came out of her house, but as she was just going to the woodpile, she didn't lock the door this time. The fox slunk away from the back of the woodpile just as she bent down at the front to pick up a piece of wood for her fire.

Then he slunk into her house and hid behind the door. When the little hen came back in and shut the door and locked it, *snick-snack*, and put the little key in her pocket, she turned to take the piece of wood to the fire.

And there was the fox holding his tote bag. She was so frightened, she dropped the piece of wood and flew straight up to the beam across the ceiling. There she sat till she'd caught her breath, then called to the fox below, "You can stay down there forever, but you won't catch me up here."

But the fox already had a trick, and it was this: He twirled and whirled in a circle after his own tail till he was going so fast, he was just a blur. And the little hen watching from above grew so dizzy, she fell right off the beam, *ker-plump!* into his tote bag. So he picked up the bag and raced over the hill to home.

But it was a high, high hill, and going down it with nothing in the bag had been easy. But climbing back with a full bag was harder. And soon the fox had to take a rest.

Inside the bag the little hen had recovered from her dizzy spell. Remembering the scissors in her pocket, she cut a little hole in the bag, *snip-snap*, and stuck her head out.

Oh my! They were more than halfway up the hill! She could hear the fox huffing and puffing nearby. She poked her head out a bit more. Not only was he huffing and puffing, he was taking a nap and snoring.

Well, the little hen made the hole bigger, and out she climbed. Then she found a nice stone just her size, and she popped it into the fox's bag as quick as could be. What a clever little hen!

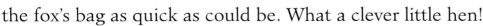

Then off she ran home and locked the door behind.

The fox woke from his nap, hefted the bag, which seemed even heavier than before, and carried it to his den, where his old mother waited.

"Mother of mine," he called, "take the lid off the pot and I will pop the hen right in. We will have a grand supper tonight, that I can tell you."

So she took off the lid and he gave the bag a shake.

Out fell the stone and landed in the boiling water with an enormous *SPLISH- SPLASH!* Boiling water spilled out on the fox and his greedy mother. And they never went after the little hen again.

Be careful around hidden stones—
They may drop out and scald your bones.

NOAH'S ARK
(Israel/Old Testament)

nce long ago, when the world was relatively new, the people had become mean and horrible to one another.

So God decided to punish them. But there was one good man and his family, and all the innocent animals, that God wished to save.

So God called down to that good man, Noah, in a voice that was bigger than the world but soft enough not to break Noah's eardrums.

He said, "Noah, I am going to flood the world, but I want you to build an ark. It shall be three stories high, with stables and rooms. And you will bring in two by two all the birds and animals and creatures who live both on the ground and below it, as well as birds that fly in the sky and all other winged creatures, though the fish and whales you may leave in the sea, for they already make their homes there."

"An ark?" Noah asked. He'd never built an ark before. Never even seen one. But God gave him instructions, and so Noah began.

For months Noah and his wife, his three sons, and their three wives hammered and sawed and decorated the ark. And even though people jeered at what he was doing, and called him silly names, and some even threw rotten vegetables at the ark, no one else volunteered to help. They were not nice people at all.

As soon as the ark was finished, Noah and his wife and his sons and their wives put in food for all who would join them—grain and oats, wheat and grass, meat and milk—until the storerooms were full.

Then they began to gather in the animals. Two by two the beasts were shepherded in. Cats and dogs, rats and mice, deer and rabbits, lions and horses, in they came and were put in their stalls. Zebras and emus, jackals and starlings, bears, lynx, ravens, wolves, wapiti, and doves.

On and on they came, slithering and walking and hopping and running, until at last the ark was full. The wild beasts were on the lowest level. The tame beasts and the birds were on the second level. The humans—Noah and his family—lived on the top.

And then it began to rain.

The rain fell for forty days and forty nights. Puddles became streams. Streams became rivers. Rivers became oceans. And the ark began to float.

Farms were drowned. Villages were drowned. Towns were drowned. Great cities were drowned. Even the tallest mountains were drowned, and still the rain fell, until at last the earth was covered and only the ark floated, and Noah steered it, looking for a place to land.

In the seventh month after the rains had abated, the earth slowly began to emerge from the seas. The first place was the very top of Mount Ararat. But Noah didn't know where that was, and he sent out a raven to fly as far as it could to find land. The raven circled for a full day and a full night and came back exhausted. Noah then knew that for the tired raven there'd been nowhere but the ark on which to land.

Next Noah sent out a dove, and it circled for a full day and night, returning with an olive branch in its beak. So now Noah knew that somewhere there was dry land.

The next day he sent out the dove again and began to follow it. This time the dove did not return, but Noah's sons called out that they could see a bit of land rising up above the waters. And that bit of land was Mount Ararat. And there the ark landed.

When at last the waters had all subsided, God spoke to Noah again, in that great voice, saying, "Send the beasts out."

So Noah did.

When the beasts had all found homes on the land, Noah and his family came out of the ark and made homes for themselves, where they tilled the soil and the sons began their own families with their wives. The beasts had babies too. The world was reborn.

"Noah," God told him, "I will never again send a flood to cover the earth." As a sign to Noah of his promise, God set the rainbow in the sky.

If you look carefully when the sun comes out after every rain, you can see this sign still.

God gave Noah the rainbow sign
A promise that all things were fine.

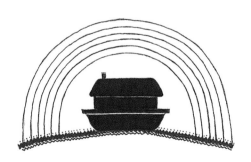

THE SOW, THE MARE, AND THE COW

(Jane Yolen)

Not so very long ago a sow, a mare, and a cow were friends. They lived together on a farm in a green and pleasant land.

One day the sow said to her friends, "I am tired of man and his fences. I want to see the world." She grunted so loudly, all the other animals heard her and turned their backs. But her friends did not.

"I agree," said the mare.

"And I," said the cow.

So that very night the mare and cow leaped over the fence and the sow crawled under. Then, one hoof after another, they went off to see the world.

But the world was full of men and fences all down the road.

The sow shook her head. "I am going into the woods," she said.

"I agree," said the mare.

"And I," said the cow.

So they pushed through branch and bramble and briar till the way grew dark and tangled. At last they found a small clearing where no fence had ever been built and no man had ever dwelled. They settled there for the night.

The sow and the mare took turns standing guard, but the cow fell right to sleep.

Then the mare began to nod. Next the sow. Soon all three were snoring, and no one was left on guard.

Suddenly a low growling filled the forest.

The sow and mare woke up with a start. The cow lowed in alarm and hid her eyes with her hooves.

The growling got louder.

The cow jumped up. Back to back, the three friends spent the rest of the night awake and trembling.

In the morning the sow said, "I think we should build a barn. Then we will be safe from the night growlers."

"I agree," said the mare.

"And I," said the cow.

So they gathered twigs and boughs, limbs and logs, leaves and moss. And soon they had built a fine, tight barn.

That night the three friends went into their barn. The sow and mare took turns standing guard, but the cow fell right to sleep.

The mare began to nod.

Then the sow.

And soon all three were asleep. No one was left awake to be the guard in the new, fine barn.

Suddenly a high howling filled the forest around them.

The sow and mare woke up with a start. The cowed lowed in alarm and tried to hide in a corner of the barn.

The howling got higher, closer.

The sow ran to guard the door. The mare ran to guard the window. The cow turned her face to the wall. And all three spent the rest of the night awake and trembling.

In the morning the sow said, "I think we need a high fence around our fine barn to keep away the night growlers and howlers."

"I agree," said the mare.

"And I," said the cow.

So they gathered logs and stumps, boulders, rocks, and stones and built themselves a high fence. They spent that night inside their fine barn inside their high fence.

Again the sow and the mare took turns standing guard, but the cow fell right to sleep.

Then the mare began to nod.

And the sow.

Soon all three were fast asleep, and no one was left awake to stand guard.

Suddenly there was a scratching at the door and a scrabbling on the roof. The sow and mare awoke with a start. The cow lowed in alarm and fell to her knees. They waited all night for someone or something to enter, but nothing did.

In the morning the three friends looked tired and pale and a little uncertain. And then the cow spoke.

"I have a sudden, great longing for man and his fences."

But the mare did not say, "I agree."

And the sow did not say, "And I."

They were suddenly much too busy digging ditches, mending roofs, tearing down the fence, and laying a path to their door.

So the cow put one hoof in front of the other all the way back to the farm in the green and pleasant land, where she lived a long and carefree life within man's fences.

As for the mare and the sow, they opened their door that very night to the howlers and

growlers, the scratchers and scrabblers, who were the forest folk come to make them welcome. And they, too, lived long and happy lives within fences of their own making.

And if you can tell which one of the three was the happiest, you are a better judge of animals than I.

Make a friend or make a fence,
Live the life that makes most sense.

The Determined Tortoise
and the World's Wisdom
(West Africa)

Once in the long ago, Ijapa the Tortoise decided he was surely the wisest creature in the whole universe. He set out to prove it to all the others. But first he knew he would have to gather all the wisdom in the world for himself so that no one could challenge him.

That very day he started around the world collecting all the wisdom he could find. Of course being a tortoise, it was slow going. But he was determined.

As he traveled, he stored every bit of wisdom he would find into a large gourd, which he hung around his neck. That made him even slower. But he was determined.

He went east and he went west. He went to the mountains and down to the valleys. To the oceanside, and the farmlands, and the cities as well. When at last he was sure that he was done collecting, he decided to hide the gourd. He whispered to himself, "Otherwise someone might steal the wisdoms and use them before I get the chance." On that point he was determined.

He saw a very tall palm tree on a beautiful beach. "I will hide the gourd at the top of that tree," he thought to himself. "No one will find it there." Then he hung the gourd on his neck like the jewel that it was and so he could keep his eye on it as he climbed. Then he tied a rope around himself and the tree, and began to haul himself up. It was very hard work—but he was determined.

However, he made very little progress because he'd get a foot or two up the tree, and slide right back down again. Another foot up, and slide down again. The gourd was rubbed and rubbed almost to the breaking point. But Ijapa the Tortoise was determined.

Just then Snail was passing by, if anything, slower than Ijapa the Tortoise. He saw Ijapa the Tortoise with the gourd around his neck, the rope around his shell, inching up and sliding back down. Inching up, and sliding back down. And Snail thought, *Ijapa the Tortoise is very determined.*

But he also knew that Tortoise was going about the climb all wrong. "Why not hang the gourd behind you instead of hanging it in front?" he asked.

Ijapa the Tortoise thought a minute, and then did as Snail suggested. After that, he easily climbed to the top of the tree. But at the top, he began to weep. "Here I thought myself so wise, yet Snail has proved himself wiser." He threw the gourd unto the ground where it broke into several pieces. And *split, splat, splot!* all the wisdom escaped back into the world.

It was that determined.

Know that wisdom is never confined
Just to the one with the wisest mind.

Tales
of
Magic Makers

SILLY WISHES
(Sweden)

Once long ago an old woman was alone in her house making a supper of bread and butter for her husband, who was out chopping wood.

There was a knock at the door, and in came a young woman as lovely as the day. Now, one needs to be careful when young women lovely as the day come knocking on one's door at suppertime. Who knows what mischief can happen then?

"May I borrow some butter?" asked the young woman.

"Of course," the old woman said, without thinking twice.

So the young woman took the butter and, as she went out the door, turned. "Because of your kindness, I grant you and your husband three wishes. But be careful—even good folk come to harm if they do not think long and hard about those wishes." And just like that, she was gone.

Now remember, I did warn you about such young women. They are almost always fairies. And fairy wishes, if not well thought through, can be nothing but trouble.

The old woman did not think twice before she made her first wish. "I'd love a big, fat sausage to go with the bread and butter!"

And *zzzzzzzap!* Just like that, a sausage as juicy as an orange appeared in the frying pan.

Just then the old woman's husband came home, tired and hungry, and she told him the story and showed him the sausage simmering in its juices in the pan.

The old man yelled, "Foolish old woman, why don't you think before you speak? You could have wished for anything in the world— gold, jewels, a big house—and you only wished for a sausage?" He shook with rage and didn't think twice himself. "Well, I wish that silly sausage was stuck to your nose."

With a *zzzzzzzap!* and a *sizzzzzle!* the fat sausage flew out of the pan and stuck right to the end of the old woman's nose. She pulled at it and pushed at it and slapped at it, but she couldn't get it off. The sausage was stuck there fast.

The old woman screamed and hollered and cried, "Do something!  Do something! How can I live the rest of my life with a sausage on the end of my nose!"

Well, he thought not once, not twice, but for the rest of the evening. He thought about wishing for a pocket full of gold, or a new house with a big new stove that would keep them warm all winter, but in the end he could not help feeling awful every time he glanced at the sausage stuck to his wife's nose.

So in the end he said, "I wish that sausage be gone from your nose and back in the frying pan, where it belongs."

And no sooner said than done. The old woman's nose was fine. The sausage finished cooking in the frying pan. And the old man and the old woman had the best dinner ever.

Wishes are fine, but who is the winner
If wishes end up being eaten for dinner?

THE SHOEMAKER AND THE ELVES
(Germany)

There was once a poor shoemaker and his poor wife. They lived in a poor house and had a poor business.

In fact, business was so poor that all he had left was enough leather to make one pair of shoes.

"Poor us," said the shoemaker that evening. "After this, whatever shall become of us?"

"You can only do what you can," said his wife. "Cut out the patterns, say your prayers, and come to bed."

So the shoemaker did as she said. He cut out a pattern for a pair of boots, knelt at his prayers, and then went to sleep. They did not wake up till morning light.

The shoemaker got out of bed and went to his workroom, ready to start on the boots. But when he got there, what did he find but a pair of boots so beautifully sewn, he could never have made the likes of them.

"Wife! Wife!" he called, and there was such wonder and fear in his voice, she ran in from the kitchen, where she had been making their poor breakfast of milk and bread.

When she saw the boots with their tiny, perfect stitches, she shook her head. "Maybe," she said, "this is the answer to our prayers."

And perhaps it was, because just then a customer came into the shop, saw the boots, and was so pleased with them, he paid far more than the usual price.

There was enough money for the shoemaker to buy leather for two more pairs of shoes, and a bit of sausage for the next morning's meal as well.

That evening he cut out the patterns for the two pairs of shoes, said his prayers, and went to bed. He and his wife snored all through the night.

The next morning, as his wife cooked sausage in the kitchen, the shoemaker went into his workshop and there were two perfect pairs of shoes with the tiny, beautiful stitches. The first two customers who came into the shop bought the shoes for far more than he would have asked, and this time there was enough money for leather for four pairs of shoes, as well as cheese and sausage and bread and tea.

And so it went. Each night the shoemaker cut out the leather patterns and the next morning found shoes that had been made as if by magic. One customer told another, and soon the shoemaker and his wife were rich beyond their wildest dreams.

But their good fortune troubled the shoemaker and his wife. They didn't know if it was a good spirit or a wicked one watching over them. So they decided together to stay up all night and watch.

They cut out the patterns together—for now there was too much work for just the shoemaker on his own—and said their prayers, got into their bedclothes, and pretended to go to sleep. But long before the church bells had rung the midnight hour, they sneaked through the darkened house to stand behind the workshop curtains to watch.

Just at midnight they heard *thump* and *bump*, and out of a mousehole crawled two little men, naked as newborns. They got right to work,  stitching and sewing, hammering and nailing, until the church bells rang out six o'clock. Then they set the newly made shoes on the shoemaker's table and disappeared back into the mousehole with not a word spoken the entire night.

"Those little men have made us rich, Husband," said the wife. "Yet they have nothing for themselves."

"Let us make them tiny shirts and pants and shoes so they will not freeze to death, poor mites," her husband answered.

So they worked all day to make the gifts and set them out by the new leather patterns that night. Then, saying their prayers, they went to bed, this time to sleep.

But right at midnight, after the bells had tolled, the shoemaker and his wife were awakened by a commotion in the workshop. There was laughing and singing and a strange caterwauling. They got out of bed and tiptoed down the hall.

The little men were dressed in their new clothes and shoes, and they were dancing about, singing.

"Look at us, dressed for the day,
We'll make no shoes, we are away!"

And off they danced across the table, jumped to the floor, ran into the mousehole, and were gone. They never returned.

The shoemaker and his wife were not sad, because they'd paid the elves in kind for all their hard work. And in fact, their customers continued to double and triple, so the shoemaker and his wife did, indeed, live happily ever after.

A kindness done, in kind returned,
Gives happiness to all concerned.

STONECUTTER

(Japan)

Once long ago there lived a stonecutter. He went every day to a great rock in the side of a mountain and cut slabs for gravestones or statues or houses. He was a careful workman and he had plenty of customers.

Though the stonecutter didn't know it, a spirit lived in the mountain that now and then helped good people to become rich and prosperous, or to otherwise lead them to great happiness.

Now, one day as the stonecutter carried a large slab of gray stone into a rich man's house, he noticed all sorts of beautiful things there. And though he'd never been jealous of such riches before, he found himself sighing. "Oh, if only I were a rich man, and could sleep in a teak bed with silken curtains and golden tassels, how happy I should be!"

And a strange, whispery voice answered him. "Your wish is heard, Stonecutter. A rich man you shall be!"

The stonecutter looked around but could see nobody and thought a trick was being played on him. So he picked up his tools and went home, still dreaming of all the beautiful things he'd seen in the rich man's house.

When he came to his own little house, he stopped, amazed. Instead of his wooden hut there stood a stately palace filled with new teak furniture. Most splendid of all was a teak bed with the very tassels and silken curtains he'd seen in the rich man's house. The stonecutter wept with happiness, and in a moment his old life was forgotten.

It was now the beginning of summer. One morning was so hot, the stonecutter could scarcely breathe as he lay dozing on his bed. He heard a noise in the street and peeped around the blinds. A carriage was passing by, drawn by six servants dressed in red and gold. In the carriage sat a prince, and over his head a golden umbrella was held by a footboy, to protect the prince from the sun.

"Oh," whispered the stonecutter, "if only I were a prince in such a carriage with a golden umbrella held over me, how powerful and happy I should be!"

And in that very instant a prince he was. Before his carriage rode a company of fierce-looking guards, with another company of guards behind. And above his head a footboy held the very umbrella he'd wanted.

But suddenly the stonecutter realized that in spite of the carriage and the umbrella over his head, in spite of the two companies of

guards, there was something mightier than he, and it
spoiled his happiness. "The sun," he cried, "oh, if only
I were the sun!"

And in that very moment he became the sun.

The stonecutter felt his heat and his power. He scorched the earth
with his rays. He browned the faces of princes and poor folk alike.

But then a cloud passed between him and the earth, and he began
to sulk. "The cloud is mightier than I am. Oh, I wish I were a cloud."

The very moment he said that, he was indeed a cloud, a gray cloud
lying between the sun and the earth. He caught up the sun's beams,
 and to his great joy, doing so allowed the earth
to grow green again. Flowers blossomed. "How
powerful I am now," he told himself. He poured
rain down till rivers overflowed their banks, and the rice plants stood
knee-deep in water. Towns and villages were destroyed by the power of
the rain; only the great rock on the mountainside remained unmoved.

The cloud who had been the stonecutter cried out, "Is the rock,
then, mightier than I? Oh, if only I were that rock!"

And in that moment he was the rock, standing
proudly, unmoving, supremely powerful. The sun
did not burn him, the rain could not move him.

"Now I am the mightiest of all!"

But one day he heard a loud noise at his feet, and looking down,
he saw a stonecutter with chisel and hammer pounding into his stone
surface. A trembling ran through him as a great block of himself broke
off and fell upon the ground.

"Is a mere man mightier than a rock? Oh, if only I were such a one!" he cried out.

In that very moment he was that man, a stonecutter, standing with his chisel and hammer at the rock foot. The stonecutter looked around—at the mountain, at the block of stone, at the path that led to his small house and his hard bed, to his poor dinner waiting for him there. But in that moment he knew that he didn't long to be something or somebody else. He was happy at last.

"Thank you, mountain spirit," he said, and meant every word.

Rich man, poor man, sun, cloud, stone,
Sometimes best is what is known.

ALI'S WRETCHED SACK

(Iran/A Sufi Story)

O nce a man named Ali was walking along the road into town. He was carrying a tattered sack, and all the while moaning, groaning, and complaining.

A mullah heard him and said, "What is wrong, my friend?"

Ali moaned and groaned some more. Then he held up the sack. "See this miserable thing?"

The mullah nodded.

"All that I own barely fills half this wretched sack," said Ali. "My life is not worth living."

The mullah laughed. "Maybe so," he said, snatching up the bag and running down the road. Dust from his feet swept back into Ali's eyes. Soon the mullah ran around a bend and was lost from sight.

Ali was so stunned at what had just happened, he burst into tears.

"Now I am even more unfortunate than before," he cried. He didn't even have the energy to run after the mullah, but plodded along the road.

Now, when the mullah had run around the bend, he stopped and placed Ali's sack in the middle of the road where Ali would soon come upon it. Then the mullah stepped behind a bush to wait.

One foot in front of another, Ali eventually came around the bend. And what should he see there but his old sack sitting in the road. He began a little dance, and laughed out loud. "Oh my pretty sack! I thought you were gone forever!"

The mullah watching this from behind a bush chuckled. "See how you can make someone happy with a single wretched sack?"

When everything seems lost for good,
Good returns a happy mood.

THE TWO NEIGHBORS
(France)

nce in old France two neighbors lived on opposite sides of a country lane.

One neighbor lived in a large house. She had piles of gold coins that she kept in little jars in every room in the house. But she never gave anything to those in need.

The other neighbor lived in a small house. In fact, it was little more than a hut. But she was happy all day long and always gave something to anyone who asked.

Now, one afternoon a beggar came through the village and knocked at the rich neighbor's door. When she opened it and saw who it was, she shut the door in his face.

The beggar shrugged. He had met people like her before. Rich on the outside, poor within. He went across the lane and knocked on the little hut.

The door opened and the woman told him to come in. She gave him half of her only loaf of bread with some butter and jam, plus some of her jug of milk.

The beggar smiled, and it was a beautiful smile. Almost—one might say—the smile of an angel.

"A meal fit for the king himself," he said to her. "And given with a good heart. Is there anything I can give you in return?"

She smiled back. "I have nothing I need."

"Nevertheless," he said, "you must let me make you this wish: Whatever you do first thing tomorrow morning, may you do all the rest of the day."

It seemed an odd wish, but the good woman thought no more of it and waved as the beggar vanished down the lane into the night.

The next morning the good woman woke and, without remembering what the beggar had wished for her, got right to work. She sat down at the spinning wheel and spun and spun and spun, faster than she ever had in her life, and she worked without stopping all day long. She never felt tired or hungry, and she did not ache anywhere, which was strange indeed.

When at last it was night, she stood and looked at the thread she had spun. It was more beautiful and stronger than any she had ever spun before. She was able to sell it all the next day to the queen's own dressmaker for so much money, she did not have to worry about money ever again. And then she remembered what the stranger had said.

Of course, a village being a village, by day's end and the market's close everyone knew about the good woman's wonderful luck and the wish the stranger had made for her. And everyone was happy for her, because she had helped out each one of them over the years. Well, *almost* everyone was happy.

The rich woman was furious. She raged for one and two and three days, until, by chance, the beggar passed by again.

When she saw him out of the window, walking down the lane, she ran outside and grabbed him by the arm.

"I am so sorry," she said, though her voice didn't say so. She dragged him inside and gave him a full meal—meat and salad and bread and wine.

When he had finished eating, he said, as he had before to her neighbor, "A meal fit for the king himself." He smiled. "Is there anything I can give you in return?"

She looked at him and smiled back. "Just the same blessing you gave my neighbor," she said.

"That seems fair," he said. "So, whatever you do first thing tomorrow morning, may you do all the rest of the day."

She smiled again and rushed him out of the door. Then she climbed into bed and began to think about what she would do when she woke. "I will not spin or sew or cook or clean the house," she told herself.

"But what should I do?" And then she sat up in bed. "I know! I will count gold coins all day long." She rose and got out one of her jar of coins and put it by the bed so she would not have far to go. Then she fell into a deep, dreamless sleep.

In the morning, before the rooster crowed, the rich lady got out of bed. She was about to reach into the jar of coins when a flea bit her on the ear. Without thinking, she reached up and scratched her ear. The flea moved down to her neck, so she scratched there.

The rooster crowed, and the flea moved again, this time to the other ear. No, not that flea, but another. And another. And another. She scratched again.

All day long, until night came, the woman scratched and scratched and tried to get rid of the fleas. By evening she was exhausted, but not too exhausted to hear the laughter of the villagers. She was so embarrassed and so upset that she ran out of the house and was never seen again.

A wish twice made might not agree;
There's just one letter between "flea" and "flee."

THE GOLDEN GOOSE

(Germany/Brothers Grimm)

nce there was a man and his wife who had three sons: Hans, Klaus, and Dummling. Everybody laughed at Dummling and swore he was as stupid as his name.

One day Hans went into the forest to cut wood. His mother had given him a sweet cake and a bottle of wine for his lunch.

Halfway into the forest he met a bent old man.

"Good day," said the old man. "Can you give me something to eat and drink? I've eaten nothing since yesterday."

Hans shook his head. "If I give away my cake and wine, I'll have nothing for myself." He walked away. But when he began to cut down a birch tree, suddenly the ax slipped and cut his arm so badly, he had to run home to have it sewn up.

"Aha!" said the old man, who had seen it all. "That's one."

The very next day Klaus went into the forest to cut wood. His mother gave him a cake and a bottle of beer.

The little old man met Klaus in the forest and begged for something to eat and drink.

Klaus answered as Hans had: "If I give away my cake and beer, I'll have nothing for myself!" And he walked away. When he began to cut down an ash tree, his ax slipped. He cut his leg so deeply, he limped home to get it sewn up.

"Aha!" said the old man, who'd been watching. "That's two."

So Dummling said to his father, "Let me go and cut down the tree we need."

His father answered: "You don't understand anything about cutting wood. You'll likely cut your head off!"

But Dummling begged so long that at last his father gave in. "Perhaps you'll learn something."

His mother gave him a cinder cake and a bottle of warm water.

When Dummling got to the forest, there was the old man.

"Can you give me something to eat and drink? I've had nothing for three days."

"I've only cinder cake and warm water, sir, but if you can stomach that, we can sit down together."

The old man smiled. "That's the best offer I've had."

Wonder of wonders, when Dummling pulled out his cinder cake, it was large and sweet. The water had become a pitcher of cold milk.

So they ate and drank, and when they were both full,

the old man said, "You were willing to divide what little you had, so I'll give *you* good luck. There"—he pointed—"stands an old tree. If you cut it down, you'll find a surprise at the roots." Then he turned around three times and disappeared.

Dummling did as he was told, and at the roots sat a goose with golden feathers. He lifted up the goose and trotted off to a nearby inn.

Now, the innkeeper had three daughters who each wanted one of the golden feathers. As soon as Dummling went into the kitchen, the eldest grabbed hold of the goose's wing.

Wonder of wonders, her hand stuck fast.

Then the second daughter tried to get a golden feather for herself. She pushed her sister out of the way. But the moment she touched her sister, she was stuck fast as well.

When the third came close, the others cried, "Keep away, keep away!" But she thought they wanted the feather for themselves, and pushed the second sister out of her way. And so she, too, got stuck fast.

Did Dummling notice? Not a bit. He ate his meal and went to bed and in the morning took the goose under his arm and set out, the greedy sisters—stuck as they were—running behind.

Now as Dummling passed a field, the village priest saw them and scolded, "For shame, you silly girls, running after this young man." He grabbed the youngest by the hand to pull her away. But of course the moment he touched her, he was stuck as well.

Then a donkey driver came along and tried to help. And he was stuck. Two laborers in the field tried. And they were stuck.

A miller, carpenter, soldier, and thief—they all became stuck, trotting one after another behind Dummling, though he never noticed.

So that was twelve of them going along the road. What a sight they were!

Before long they came to the royal city, where the king's lovely daughter could not laugh. The king had decreed that whoever made her laugh could marry her and be king himself thereafter.

The princess happened to be looking out her window when the eleven people running stuck together after Dummling and his golden goose came into view. She began to giggle. Then to guffaw. Finally, she roared with laughter.

And Dummling—who was not so dumb as all that—immediately went to the throne room, with the eleven people behind him.

"I would like to marry the laughing princess," he said.

Well, the king looked at Dummling and he made all kinds of conditions.

"First," said the king, "you must find someone to drink a cellarful of wine."

Dummling thought at once of the hungry old man in the forest. Leaving the golden goose and all the people stuck to it with the princess, he went back to find him sitting on the stump of the tree where the golden goose had been. The old man was weeping.

"Why are you crying?" asked Dummling.

"I've such a great thirst that I've drunk up a barrel of wine and am still not full," he answered.

"Why, I know just the thing," said Dummling, leading him back to the castle cellar. There the old man drank and drank till he'd emptied all the barrels of wine, and then he disappeared.

So Dummling went to the king and asked again for his bride, but the king made a new condition.

"You must find someone who can eat a whole mountain of bread."

Dummling went straight back to the forest. At the same tree was the old man. "I've eaten a whole ovenful of rolls but am still hungry."

"Why, I know just the thing," said Dummling, leading him back to the castle kitchen, where hundreds of breads had been baked. The old man began to eat and eat, till he'd eaten every bread, and then he disappeared.

So Dummling asked a third time for his bride, but the king again gave him an impossible task. "I want a ship that can sail on land and on water. As soon as you come sailing back in it, you shall marry my daughter."

Dummling went straight into the forest and found the old man again. When he heard what Dummling wanted, the old man said: "I'll give you that ship because three times already you've been kind to me."

When Dummling sailed out of the forest and down the road and up to the castle gate in the ship, the king could no longer prevent the marriage. The moment Dummling and the princess said "I do," the spell on the golden goose was broken, and all the people who'd been stuck fast danced at their wedding.

Years later, after the king's death, Dummling inherited the kingdom and lived for a long time contentedly with his wife, his ten children, and the golden goose.

A goose will often take you far,
From where you were to where you are.

THE MERMAN'S SOCK
(Denmark)

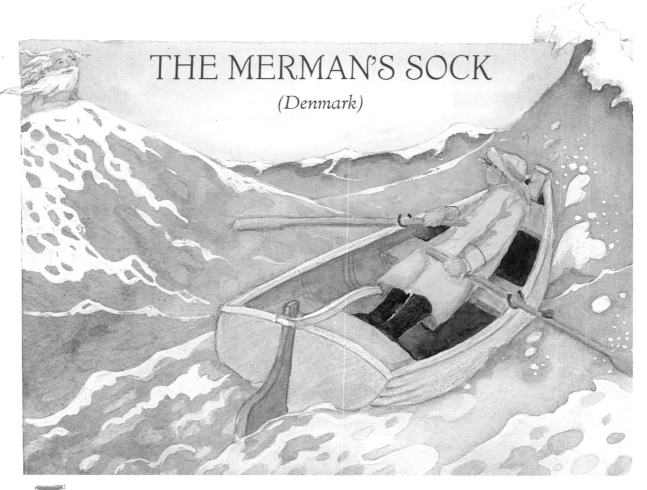

It was a cold, cold winter's day when a fishmerman named Hans put out to sea. The wind began to whip around his little boat, and he thought he'd better return home. But it was blowing so hard, Hans didn't think he'd make it.

All of a sudden, ahead of him, he saw the strangest sight—an old man with a long white beard was coming straight toward him, riding along on the very top of a wave, with no boat beneath him.

A merman! thought Hans. He knew that meant a huge storm was coming.

"Oh, brrrr," said the merman, "how cold it is." He held up one foot to show Hans he'd lost his right sock. His foot was blue as ice.

Now, Hans also knew that mermaids all have fish tails, but not all mermen do. At once he stripped off his own right boot, took off his sock, and threw it to the merman, for what was the use of a sock to him if he was to go down with his little boat in a storm?

The merman grabbed the sock and dived to the bottom of the sea, and immediately the sea grew calm. Hans was able to row safely home.

His wife scolded him for losing his sock, for it meant she would have to knit another one. But when he told her whom he'd given it to, she said, "Then blessings, my old man. That merman won't forget."

A few months passed and Hans was out again on the sea. Suddenly two greenish hands appeared on his gunwale, near his oars. Then up popped the same old merman, seaweed in his beard.

"Lost another sock?" asked Hans.

But the merman answered him this way:

"Turn about, sock man, escape the fray.
There's thunder and storms over all Norraway."

Hans nodded. He didn't have to be told twice. Calling out his thanks, he hurried back to shore as fast as he could row. No sooner had he pulled his boat up onto the beach than a huge storm hit, greater than any he'd seen in his long life. Lightning struck all about, the thunder was as loud as kettledrums, and waves the size of mountains rose and fell and rose again.

Many boats were lost that day at sea. But Hans the fisherman had gotten home safe because he'd given the merman a sock for his icy foot.

Here is how this fish tale ends:
The merfolk don't forget their friends.

HOW ANANSI SPIDER
GOT ALL HIS STORIES
(Africa)

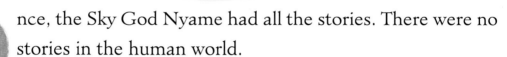

nce, the Sky God Nyame had all the stories. There were no stories in the human world.

But Anansi Spider loved stories and he wanted to give them to the humans. So he went to the Sky God and asked, "How much will it cost to buy your stories?"

Nyame did not want to sell them, but it was impolite not to set a price. So he made it a very big price. Smiling, he said, "Bring me back Onini Python, Osebo Leopard, the Mmoboro Hornets, and Mmoatia, the dwarf." He said it with great seriousness, but inside he was laughing because he knew this was an impossible task.

Anansi did not believe *anything* was impossible. "'Impossible' is only two letters away from 'possible'," he told himself. He was a tricky kind of creature. He knew with good tricks he could get some of those creatures for the Sky God. But the biggest trick would be to get them all.

First he went to the forest where Onini Python lived. It was dark and tangled in those woods. When he found the great tree where the snake was stretched out, Anansi didn't look up. Instead he stood under the branch and spoke aloud as if talking to himself.

"Really," Anansi said, "I don't think that Python is truly longer than the palm branch. That's too hard to believe. It's just his shadow that's long."

Python overheard. He swung his great neck down until he was eye to eye with Anansi, and said, "What do you mean I'm not that long?"

"Prove it," Anansi said. "There is the branch. Stretch out."

Onini Python stretched and stretched, but a snake likes to curl and coil, and so he was never perfectly straight.

"Let me help," said Anansi. "I will tie you to the branch, and then I can measure. I am sure you are right."

So Python agreed to be tied to the branch.

As soon as Python was secure, Anansi took out a saw and cut down the branch and carried the branch to the Sky God, singing:

"Here is one.
I've almost won!"

The Sky God laughed. "There are still three more to go," he said.

So Anansi went to the woods where Osebo Leopard lived and dug a deep hole in the ground. He covered it with grasses so it looked as if no hole was there. Then he waited quietly in a tree until Leopard came strolling along.

Anansi called down, "Osebo Leopard, I bet you can't catch me."

Leopard looked up. And since he wasn't looking down, he stepped right onto the grasses that covered the hole, and *kabump!* Down he went. At the bottom of the hole he howled and yowled.

"Oh dear, oh dear, I didn't know that hole was there," said Anansi Spider. "Let me help you out, dear friend." He threw down his webs.

"Thank you," Leopard said, and stepped onto the webs. Anasi hauled him out. But once up on the path, Leopard realized he was caught fast in the sticky webs.

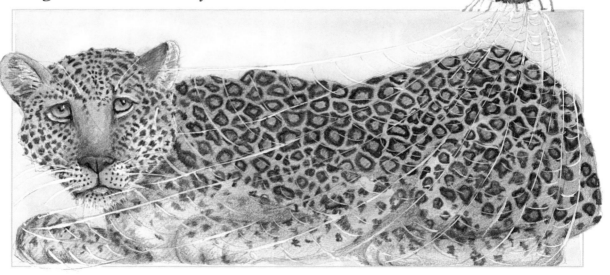

Anansi tied Leopard firmly and brought him to the Sky God, singing:

"Here is two,
I'm almost through."

The Sky God laughed. "There are still two more to go," he said.

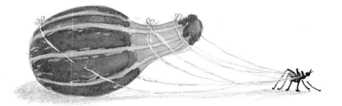

Now it was time to catch the Mmoboro Hornets. Very tricky, as there were so many of them. So Anansi filled a calabash—a great hollow gourd—with water. He poured some of the water over a banana leaf he held over his head, and even more over the Mmoboro Hornets' nest.

"Oh Brother Hornets," he called, "it's raining so hard, I'm afraid you'll drown."

"Can you save us, Brother Spider?" the hornets cried back.

"I'll do what I can," Anansi told them. "Why look, here's an empty calabash. Why don't you climb in and I'll take you to safety?"

So they did just that, and when the very last was inside, Anansi sealed up the opening with wax and ran with it to the Sky God, singing:

"Here is three
Of your tough fee."

The Sky God laughed. "There is still one more to go," he said.

Anasi thought long and hard about how to catch Mmoatia, the dwarf. At last he decided to make a doll and cover it with sticky gum. Then he put the doll under the odum tree, which was where the dwarfs liked to play. Finally, he placed a bowl filled with yams in front of the doll.

Soon Mmoatia came to the odum tree. Seeing the yams in the bowl, and feeling hungry, she ate them right up. Then she thanked the doll.

Well, of course the doll said nothing back, which, as it was a doll, made sense. But Mmoatia had very bad eyesight and didn't know it was a doll. She thought it was a young person with poor manners.

"Have you nothing to say to me in return?" asked Mmoatia.

Of course the doll *still* didn't reply.

Annoyed, Mmoatia struck the gum doll, first with one hand, then with the other. Her hands stuck in the sticky gum, and Anansi ran back with her over his shoulder all the way to the Sky God, singing:

"Here is four,
I need no more."

"Indeed you do not," said the Sky God as he handed Anansi all the stories. And that is how tricksy Spider Anansi got to own all the stories of the world, and you now have heard the very first one.

If you want to hear a tale,
Find a spider without fail.

THE SWEET PORRIDGE POT

(Germany/Brothers Grimm)

here was once a poor but good little girl who lived all alone with her sickly mother in a little hut by the forest.

They were so very poor, they had nothing left in the house to eat and had already begged what they could from their neighbors. No one wanted to help them anymore.

So the girl said to her mother, "Perhaps I shall find something in the forest for our pot."

Well, she walked and she walked through the woods and found nothing. Not a berry, not a mushroom, not a fern or flower they could eat. It was deep into November and nothing grew.

Tired and cold, her little legs aching from all that walking, she sat down on a fallen log and began to cry.

"There, there," said a kindly voice. "Nothing's ended that can't be mended."

Looking up, she saw an aged woman smiling at her.

"Oh," said the girl, "there's nothing that can mend hunger except food. And I have found nothing my poor mother and I can eat."

The old woman smiled kindly and handed the girl a little pot.

"Alas, we already have a pot. It's what goes in it we lack," said the girl. "I thank you for your kindness, though."

"Listen, my child," the old woman said, "this is no ordinary pot. Put it on the stove empty and say, 'Cook, little pot, cook.' And the pot will cook you good, sweet, wholesome, filling porridge."

"But . . . but . . . that's impossible," the girl said.

"No—that's *magic*," corrected the old woman. "But when you have enough, you must say, 'Stop, little pot, stop,' and the pot will stop cooking."

Well, the girl curtsied, took the pot, kissed the old fairy on the cheek (for of course it was a fairy), and ran back to her mother.

At once the child set the pot on the stove and said the magic words, and the pot cooked them up a big bowl of porridge. They ate and ate and for the first time in weeks were not hungry.

And so they passed the winter, always grateful for the fairy's little magic pot.

Now, if that had been the whole story, how nice this tale would be. And how short. But life is seldom that easy, and magic never.

One day in the spring the little girl went out into the woods again, for as wonderful as the porridge was, she and her mother were both longing to add something to it.

But her mother, now healthy again from all that porridge, decided to have one more helping of it. She set the pot on the stove and said, "Cook, little pot, cook."

The little pot gave a kind of sigh and set about cooking a second pot of porridge for the morning. And the mother, dipping her spoon in, ate right out of the pot until she was full. Then she turned and went into the next room to do some spinning.

Oh no! She forgot to say the words to stop the pot cooking, so it went on and on. It was magic, you see, and did not have sense on its own. So the porridge rose up, up, and up in the pot to the edge, then over the edge.

And still the little pot kept cooking.

The porridge fell onto the table, then onto the floor, more and more of it, until the kitchen and whole house were full, and then the next house, and then the whole street, just as if it wanted to satisfy the hunger of the whole world.

When the girl's mother heard the noise of the porridge filling the room, she came in and had to wade through the porridge to get to the stove. And she was so frightened and bewildered that she could not remember the proper words to make the pot stop. She shouted out things like "Stop, you silly pot!" and "Please, please, please cut it out!" and "I'm going to take a stick to you if you do not quit!"

But of course that did not stop the pot from cooking.

At last the little girl came home, her arms full of wild berries and good mushrooms. When she got to the edge of town and saw the porridge coming down the lane, she guessed what had happened. She waded up to her door and cried out, "Stop, little pot, stop!"

Of course the pot stopped.

And anyone in town who wanted to get into their house had to eat their way back in.

Magic has rules, for pots and such.
Sometimes a lot is simply too much.

BRAVE MARIETTA

(Italy)

In old Italy there was a widowed farmer who had two things he loved: his little daughter, Marietta, and his pear tree. But each summer when the pears were ripe, he had to take four baskets of them to the king as rent for his cottage and land.

Now, one year the winter had been bad, and the spring worse, and he could fill only three of the baskets. He was afraid he would lose all they had.

So, with a heavy heart, he put the pears in three of the baskets, and little Marietta, who was fast asleep, in the fourth, to bring the weight of the baskets up. Then, wheeling them in his handcart, he headed to the palace. He thought that after the baskets were weighed, he'd sneak his daughter out and take her home.

But alas, there were so many folk paying rent that day, he had to leave the baskets in the pantry and was told to come back the next day.

After a while little Marietta awoke and—oh!—she was hungry. So she ate some pears. A bit later she'd eaten up almost half the pears and fallen asleep in the pantry.

The cook saw that pears were disappearing. He searched the pantry and found the sleeping child. When he began to scold her, she wept piteously.

"Do not cry, pretty little girl," the cook said. "Come and work for me in the kitchen."

And so she did.

Eventually her father heard what had happened, and thought, *I love my daughter but cannot feed her. At least now she's in a good place.* And though it broke his heart, he knew it was for the best.

Marietta worked in the king's kitchen until she'd grown into a beautiful young maiden. She was such a good worker, everyone loved her, even the king's son. Well, perhaps not everyone. There were three servants who were jealous of her and decided to make her life miserable.

They went to the king and said, "This Marietta whom everyone praises is really a boaster. She says she can do all the palace laundry herself—wash it, dry it, iron it, and fold it away all in one morning—and that even the king couldn't do such a thing."

Well, kings hate to hear anyone boast like that. So he sent for Marietta and told her what he had been told.

Marietta smiled. "No one can do such a thing."

"Not even a king?" asked the king.

"Not even you, sire," she said. But it was the wrong thing to say.

The king said, "You must do as you've said. And if you don't, you'll be punished."

Marietta went back to the kitchen weeping bitterly. The prince found her there, and she told him what had happened.

"Dry your eyes, sweet Marietta," he said. "I'll help you. Have the king send all the dirty linen to the laundry, and I'll meet you there."

When the prince arrived, the sheets and pillowcases, tablecloths and towels, were piled up to the ceiling. He took out a wand from his

pocket and waved it, and in a moment everything was washed, dried, ironed, folded, and ready to be put away.

"Do not say who helped you," he told Marietta, and went back to his room.

The king was delighted, but the three jealous servants were not.

So they went again to the king and said, "Now Marietta is boasting she can go across the slimy river to the ogress's house and get back your box of magical instruments."

So the king sent for Marietta and told her what he'd been told.

Marietta smiled. "No one can do such a thing."

"Not even a king?" asked the king.

"Not even you, sire," she said. But it was the wrong thing to say.

The king said, "You must do as you've said. And if you don't, you'll be punished."

Marietta went back to the kitchen weeping bitterly. The prince found her there, and she told him what had happened.

"Dry your eyes, sweet Marietta," he said. "I'll help you. Ask the king for three quarts of oil and three pounds of fresh beef. And there is one thing more, which you must keep to yourself. . . ."

The king agreed, packing everything in a large bag, and off Marietta went to the slimy river.

As the prince had instructed, she knelt down and put her hands in the river, saying, "Sweet river, lovely river, if I weren't in such a hurry, I'd stop to bathe in your lovely waters."

The river was only used to being called ugly and dirty and slimy and was so happy, it pulled its water aside, saying:

"Cross over, cross over,
To my farthest shore,
Walk over as if you were
On a dry floor."

And Marietta went across.

The ogress's palace was much more beautiful than the king's, with seventeen turrets topped with gold, and marble pillars on every side.

No sooner had she gone through the palace door than up leaped three enormous dogs, each as large as a horse, barking and growling. Marietta threw them each a pound of fresh beef. Then they wagged their tails like puppies and let her pass.

Beyond her was an iron door that was so rusty, she knew that opening it would make the hinges squeak and squeal. So she poured the oil on the hinges, and then the door opened quietly.

Up the stairs Marietta crept to the ogress's bedroom, where under the bed she kept the king's box of magical instruments.

But just when Marietta was pulling the box out, the ogress awoke.

Marietta grabbed up the box and ran down the stairs, *slip-slap-tip-tap*, with the ogress running after her.

When Marietta got to the door, the ogress cried out, "Door, door, squeeze her tight."

But the door said, "For a hundred years my hinges have rusted, and you never oiled them once. Marietta has. I stay open for her." Then it stayed open till Marietta was through, and slammed itself in the ogress's face.

The ogress had to knock the door down, crying out to her guard dogs, "Dogs, dogs, bite her."

But the dogs didn't move, saying, "For a hundred years you have given us only scraps of bread, but Marietta has given us meat. We won't bite her."

Then Marietta ran to the river, and behind her the ogress cried, "River, river, drown her."

The river said, "Why should I drown her? She's the only one who didn't call me nasty names." And the river drew back its waters again and let Marietta across. Once she was across and the ogress in the middle, the river let its waters come roaring back, and the old ogress was carried away, never to be seen again.

The prince stood on the other side. He took the box with one hand and Marietta with the other. "Will you marry me, brave Marietta?"

"With all my heart," she said.

The king was pleased. The cook was pleased. The old pear farmer was pleased. And most pleased of all were the prince and Marietta. As for the jealous servants, they were quickly dismissed and, like the ogress, were never seen again.

A kind word, a bit of oil,
Can save you from a life of toil.

FROG PRINCE
(Germany/Brothers Grimm)

One evening a princess went into the wood and sat down by a well. She was playing with her favorite toy, a golden ball that her father had given her. She flung it into the air again and again, catching it each time.

But one time she *didn't* catch the ball, and it fell into the well, which was so deep, she couldn't see to the bottom.

So she began to weep and wail, crying out in a sad little voice, "Oh, if only I had my little golden ball. I would give all my fine clothes and jewels to have my little golden ball in my hand again."

With a *splish* and a *splash*, and a great big hop, a huge green frog leaped onto the rim of the well and said (remember, this is a fairy tale), "I don't want your clothes or your jewels, but if you promise to love me and feed me and let me sleep in your little bed, I'll bring it to you."

The princess was sure he couldn't do such a thing. But she was also sure that frogs couldn't talk, and here he was talking. So just in case, she said, "If you bring me back my golden ball, I'll let you have what you ask." *After all,* she thought, *how could he come to the palace to claim the reward?* It was a long way from the well, and who would let a frog in? Not the guards. Not her father.

The frog nodded as if they'd made an actual agreement, and leaped back down into the well. A moment later he came up onto the rim of the well with the golden ball in his little green hand.

The princess thanked him prettily, took the ball, and ran all the way back home.

That evening as she and her mother the queen and her father the king sat at their long table for dinner, there was a strange noise on the stairs outside the dining-room door. It went *slurp, tip, tap.*

"What is that?" asked the queen.

But the king had heard nothing.

And the princess said nothing.

Then there came a tap on the door.

"Who is that?" asked the king.

But the queen had heard nothing.

And the princess said nothing.

A strange voice called out:

"Open the door, princess dear,
To the one who waits out here.
Remember the words you and I said,
Out by the well, in the greenwood shade."

Both the king and the queen heard this, and the king said to the princess, "If this is true, open the door."

Well, she couldn't very well lie to her father, so the princess went to the door and opened it, and there was the frog.

"Who is it?" asked the king.

And she had to tell him the story.

"If you've made a promise, you must keep it," said the king.

The frog came in and hopped to the foot of the table. "Lift me up and feed me as you promised," he said.

The princess shivered.

"Lift him up," said the king.

So she lifted him up and fed him from her own golden plate until they were both done. Then she asked to be excused, and started to leave the table.

"Take me to your room as you promised," said the frog.

"Take him up," said the king.

So she took the frog in her hand and brought him to her room. She set him on a pillow next to her own pillow on the big canopied bed. And there he told her stories till they both fell asleep.

In the morning the frog wasn't there, and the princess thought, *Now I have fulfilled all, and he is gone back to his well.*

But that night at dinner the frog was back. She fed him and brought him to the little pillow in her room. He told her more stories, which she enjoyed.

In the morning, again, he was gone. And back again at night. Food by her hand, pillow on her bed. Stories long into the night.

In the morning she expected him gone.

But when she sat up, there at the foot of her bed was the handsomest prince she'd ever seen, gazing at her with large liquid green eyes.

"Who are you?" she asked, feeling herself falling in love.

"I was the frog, enchanted by an evil witch until a princess should take me from the spring and feed me by her hand and let me sleep in her own bed for three nights."

"Oh," she said, "shall we be married? I would like to hear stories each night for the rest of my life."

And it was quickly done, a royal wedding, a carriage made of glass, a trip to the prince's palace on the other side of the greenwood shade, and everyone (except the evil witch) living happily ever after.

A promise kept in the greenwood shade
Is the best kind of promise ever made.

The End

An Afterword to My Readers

In my third floor attic library I have my collection of folklore books. There are hundreds of them there, from brand-new volumes I bought from a bookstore, to old dusty out-of-print books I found at secondhand bookstores and tag sales. They are arranged on my shelves by country of origin.

Over the years I have put together more than a dozen different collections of tales—from baby books (*Once Upon a Bedtime Story*) to a collection of tales about older people (*Gray Heroes*) to stories about brave girls *(Not One Damsel in Distress)* to Christmas stories (*Hark!*) to cat folktales (*Meow!*) to a large general collection (*Favorite Folktales from Around the World*). My goal each time is to find the most tellable stories for my readers within the confines of my collection's theme.

For *Once There Was a Story* I was looking for tales that very young readers and young listeners could enjoy. Stories short enough for a bedtime read. They needed to be from around the world; tales from other cultures that were understandable for children outside of those cultures.

I read through dozens and dozens of books, skimmed others, and even looked through folk tale sites online to find the stories for this book.

I chose tales from America, England, Russia, Japan, Germany, France, Portugal, Greece, Africa, Korea, Denmark, Tibet, Ireland, Israel, and Italy. Tales about brave and foolish boys and girls, men and women, mermen, spider gods, frogs, foxes, mice, a tortoise, several hares, a grasshopper and some ants, a mean tiger, a troop of animal musicians, and a little red hen and more.

—*Jane Yolen*

My Favorite Books Used in This Collection

Abrahams, Roger. *Afro-American Folk Tales.* New York, New York: Pantheon, 1994.

Abrahams, Roger. *African American Folktales: Stories from Black Traditions in the New World.* New York, New York: Pantheon, 1999.

Afanasev, Aleksandr and Alexander Alexeieff. *Russian Fairy Tales.* New York, New York: Pantheon, 1976.

Booss, Claire, editor. *Scandinavian Folk & Fairy Tales: Tales from Norway, Sweden, Denmark, Finland & Iceland.* New York, New York: Crown Publishing, 1988.

Bushnaq, Inea. *Arab Folktales.* New York, New York: Pantheon, 1986.

deCaro, Frank. *The Folktale Cat.* New York, New York: Dorset House Publishing, 1992.

Glassie, Henry. *Irish Folktales.* New York, New York: Pantheon, 1995.

Grimm Brothers. Norbert Guterman, translator. *The Complete Grimm's Fairy Tales.* New York, New York: Pantheon, 1975.

Hearn, Lafcadio. *Japanese Fairy Tales.* New York, New York: Boni and Liveright, 1918.

Hughes, Langston and Arna Bontemps. *The Book of Negro Folklore.* New York, New York: Dodd Mead, 1958.

In-Sob, Zong, editor and translator. *Folk Tales from Korea.* New York, New York: Routledge, 1952.

Pourrat, Henri. *French Folktales.* New York, New York: Pantheon, 1989.

Ramanujan, A. K. *Folktales from India.* New York, New York: Pantheon, 1994.

Tyler, Royall. *Japanese Tales.* New York, New York: Pantheon, 1987.

Yolen, Jane. *Favorite Folktales from Around the World.* New York, New York: Pantheon, 1986.

Yolen, Jane. *Once Upon a Bedtime Story.* Honesdale, Pennsylvania: Boyds Mills Press, 1997.